Missing the Plot

∼

Paul Chadbourne

authorHOUSE®

AuthorHouse™ UK Ltd.
500 Avebury Boulevard
Central Milton Keynes, MK9 2BE
www.authorhouse.co.uk
Phone: 08001974150

© 2009 Paul Chadbourne. All rights reserved.

No part of this book may be reproduced, stored in a retrieval system, or transmitted by any means without the written permission of the author.

First published by AuthorHouse   1/8/2009

ISBN: 978-1-4389-2535-6 (sc)

Printed in the United States of America
Bloomington, Indiana

This book is printed on acid-free paper.

Prologue

I was going away to Cyprus for one reason and one reason only, and that was to write a book.

This last twelve months had been the worst year of my life and I needed to get away and seriously think how it had come to this. I needed to consider my future and to try and get some perspective on my life.

Writing a book would keep my mind occupied. I knew through past experience that if my over-active imagination was left to its own devices it would almost certainly drive me insane. I didn't know it at the time but writing the book was a cathartic experience, a much needed therapy. It helped to channel my thoughts; it helped me to understand my inner self and it helped bring real focus to my deepest desires. It changed my life.

They say that everyone has a book in them. Don't get me wrong, I'm no expert but I'm absolutely certain that this notion is totally misguided and I would wager a million pounds to prove it. First of all who are *they* and secondly how can they make such a general sweeping statement?

I come across all sorts of people in all walks of life every single day and I can absolutely guarantee that there are many of them that couldn't even string a sentence together, never mind a dozen or so chapters!

The idea that *everyone has a book in them* is simply nonsense, unless of course we're talking about books that are full of very simple three and four letter words and in many cases mainly pictures!

On the other hand, I do believe that most reasonably intelligent people have a story to tell.

Well, in a nutshell that's why I was going to Cyprus, and *this* was my story. This was my book.

My problem was that at this precise moment in time I had no idea what my story would be about, thus the title of the book. Some may argue that I've been missing the plot for most of my adult life, and quite frankly they may be right.

This was a holiday in which I hoped to find myself and hoped to find my story.

Chapter One

Once I'd made my mind up I was going to Cyprus there was no stopping me. I needed a few essential items, like a full wardrobe of modern clothes and several pairs of shoes, a travel iron, an i-pod, a new suitcase, suntan cream, a sun hat and that stuff you plug in overnight to kill the local insect life and of course the adaptors to plug them into. Nothing too much then…. This was going to be one expensive holiday!

Oh and I also needed to take my Dictaphone and a Laptop if I was going to write my book. And I *was* going to write my book.

My flight was booked for the 3rd May from East Midlands Airport to Larnaca in Southern Cyprus. This was to be the birthplace of my first book, perhaps my only book.

Time was passing by and I had just a few days to sort out my holiday shopping list. I knew I had to get on with it and a trip to the local shopping outlet was needed.

I bought a couple of pairs of shoes from an enormous shoe shop; it was almost like a supermarket just for shoes. So *this* is shopping? It was a new experience for me and the first time I'd ever bought my own shoes. I was pleasantly surprised at how much the shop assistant flirted with me. I convinced myself it was just because I'd bought two pairs. I was sure that this must have been the reason. My ever lowering confidence with the opposite sex meant I didn't consider any other reason. Perish the thought that she might have fancied me a bit!

I mentioned I was going to Cyprus on my own in a couple of days and she seemed genuinely pleased for me. I restrained myself from buying another pair of blue and white trainers. It was a close shave. After twenty odd years in Sales and Marketing I was like so many of my kind, a sucker for a good sales person. As ever I was the easiest sale in the store by a mile.

I popped next door into a clothes shop; this was like a supermarket for clothes! Shopping *is* fun! I desperately needed to sort out my failing, if not already failed wardrobe with several new casual shirts, khaki shorts and swimming attire that I deemed suitable for the warm climate ahead. As I pulled out my wallet to pay, I looked at the pretty dark haired sales assistant who was attending to me. However, it seemed I'd already lost my charm and even though I'd bought seven different items it was obvious there would be no more flirting for me today.. Not even a flicker. You can't win them all.

The weather had been shocking in the UK for most of the year and the idea of the sun on my back was very appealing. I have to say I was getting rather excited at the thought of my impending adventure. It wasn't just the thrill of being in such a wonderful part of the world. It was much more than that, I'd be doing something I'd never done before, I was going to write a book.

I was keeping myself to myself when outside the store I bumped into my niece who greeted me with her usual hug and a peck on my cheek.

'Hiya love, how's it going? Just been to the gym?'

'No, just doing a bit of clothes shopping, I'm away for a while.'

'Anywhere nice?' she enquired. 'We're off to the Maldives in two weeks.'

'Wow, good for you' I said, managing to hide a hint of jealousy and the fact that I'd just had the wind taken out of my sails. 'No, I'm off to Cyprus, but I'm really looking forward to it.' I said convincingly.

'Oh, you'll love it, we've been there loads.' she said.

I was starting to feel a little bit deflated now. I'd hardly **been anywhere**...

A couple of times to Spain and the Canaries once or twice, but compared to her and so many other people I was a globe-trotting novice.

I considered mentioning the book, but thought better of it. I just didn't want to answer the barrage of questions that were bound to follow.

'Anyway, nice to see you got to dash... loads to do.' I said at the same time as kissing her goodbye and bidding her farewell.

I realised that I needed this holiday so much. I needed to go more places... I needed to experience the world. Cyprus was a good starting point.

Chapter Two

A few days before I was due to go I arranged to have some lunch with my best mate Tony. We met in a quaint little café in Mansfield. Tony and I went back a long way and had been best friends for over thirty years.

When we'd arranged our little meeting on the phone the previous evening I'd told him I'd got some exciting news. As ever he wanted to know there and then, but I'd insisted on telling him over lunch.

I arrived at the café about ten minutes early to find Tony already there. We smiled at each other and I suggested we order some food before the lunchtime rush. We opted for the Omelette with salad each and a pot of tea to share. As soon as we arrived at our table the question came:

'So spill the beans mate, what's the big news?'

'Patience Big Toe, I'll tell you after lunch, I'm starving!' I said it with a large amount of playfulness. I loved to tease him and I knew he was desperate to know the exciting news I was about to break.

Big Toe was one of the many nicknames I had for my friend. There was also Tone, Pony and every now and again would you believe Tony? But every time I called him Tony he always looked slightly surprised as though I'd called him Tracy or Betty or something! He answered to anything though and always gave as good as he got with names for me like Big Ed, Teddy and indeed Big Ted!

As usual we scoffed our lunches in no time and I poured the tea.

'Well Tone, are you ready?'

'You and Marie aren't back together are you?' he enquired with enthusiasm.

My mind immediately left the café and I was instantly with my estranged wife. I'd seen Marie the night before for a coffee. She was going to stay with a friend for a few days and she'd come over for half an hour to see me before I went away on my adventure. As ever when the thought of Marie entered my head I had mixed feelings, joyful memories tinged with pain and emptiness.

Back in the café I answered Tony's question with a shake of my head.

'No mate, I'm going to Cyprus to write a book.'

He looked shocked and could only say one word: 'Wow!'

'Wow? Is that all you can say?'

'Actually I was talking about the Omelette!'

I wanted to smile, but I looked at him through disapproving eyes.

He went on to ask, 'anyway what the hell's it about?

'I'm gonna write a book about a man who goes to Cyprus to write a book!'

'Right!' he said in a puzzled sort of way. 'But what's it about?'

'It's about a man who goes to Cyprus to write a book, but he's missing the plot. So it's about the adventures and the frustrations he has along the way.'

'It sounds thrilling mate!' he said with more than a hint of irony.

'It might not be up your street Tone, but it's the sort of book I would read and I'm really excited about writing it.' I'm sure I must have sounded a little pissed off, because instantly my oldest friend's whole manner changed.

'Good for you mate, I'm only kidding. And Cyprus on your own? Wow!'

He smiled as I grabbed the teapot and enquired in our long held customary way, 'more tea vicar?'

We finished off the tea and ordered another pot as we talked about all sorts of other things. Twenty minutes later we had changed the world for another day.

We shook hands and just as he was leaving he said, 'anyway I hope you have a great time mate.' He quickly added, 'am I in the book by the way?'

'Don't be daft Tone; I don't want to scare off all the ladies.'

'Fuck off!' was his shameless reply. With that he smiled and turned away towards his car. I headed back to work. I had a lot of loose ends to tie up before the holiday.

That evening I had a game of badminton with another friend. Jack was one of my new badminton partners and he was just learning the game. I'd played badminton for many years and was definitely in a different league to Jack. However, even though the standard of badminton wasn't what I'd been used to, the amount of fun we had more than made up for it. Jack was highly competitive, but unfortunately his all round game was lacking in a number of key areas. He couldn't serve, his backhand was shocking and his stamina was lacking. Every now and again I would "nil him" in a game. In other words I'd win the game 21- 0. He hated it and got more and more frustrated as the game neared its conclusion, and of course the more frustrated he got, the more his game deteriorated, which taking into account his normal standard of play he could ill afford.

I couldn't help teasing him with the line, 'Jack, you're SHIT! All you'll ever win at this game is JACKSHIT!'

He cursed me back and we laughed. 'But do you think I'm improving?' he pleaded.

'Yeah, you're not quite as shit as you were.' I replied.

'Well that's good then.' I agreed that it was good and added that given time he would become even less shit! Even though I teased him terribly I always enjoyed our game and this occasion was no exception. We played a total of nine games in the hour. He won Jack-shit!

Chapter Three

On the morning of the flight I was feeling both excited and a little nervous. It's a five hour flight and overall an eight hour journey. So I knew I was going to be shattered when I arrived in Protaras, my resort destination in Cyprus.

I arrived at the airport typically early. It's one of my many annoying habits. I always arrive far too early for everything... Whether its twenty minutes too early for a business appointment or well over an hour too early for a flight check in, I'm always too early. Fortunately not in the bedroom too often... Or so I'm told!

I kid myself its better to be too early rather than too late. But deep down I wish I could relax for a little longer before the journey and not twiddle my thumbs for hours on end when I arrive at my various and varied destinations.

I don't smoke and don't do drugs, but I am addicted to being early...I put it down to the itchy feet I inherited from my Dad.

It was time to check in and the young lady attending to me seemed to be new in the job. It's only when she said enjoy your flight to Arrecefe that I realised just how new to the job she was. I had visions of my case arriving in Lanzerote with me 1000's of miles due east in Cyprus. I pointed out in a strangely casual manner the error she had made and that I would like my belongings to accompany me on this holiday flight to Larnaca. She apologised and blushed a bright scarlet red.

She interrupted the more experienced colleague to her left and was duly instructed how to override the booking and indeed correct it. I caught the eye of the colleague and we shared a smile over the mistake.

'No harm done.' the more experienced lady said. I nodded in agreement and added, 'I don't suppose it happens very often does it?' I was feeling most relieved at my narrow escape.

'No Sir, certainly not!' she said with a degree of conviction.

I almost believed her. Almost.

We boarded the plane and I scanned the area around my seat to check out my travelling companions, the ones that would have an influence on my journey. Were there any potential screaming babies or terrible tots? Were there any groups of young lads that were bound to be over loud after several beers? The coast looked pretty clear and I felt quite content at the thought of a pain free trip.

It was at that point that I realised there was still an empty seat on my inside. There I was thinking, *'perfect, I can stretch out a bit and enjoy the journey with a little more comfort.'* I thought the plane was ready for take off, I just accepted that planes don't always fill every single seat every single time they fly.

Suddenly my darkest nightmare started to play out before my very eyes.

It never seems to be straight-forward with me, if it *can* go wrong then in my experience it certainly *will* go wrong. Picture the scene, it was not pretty, but be my guest: A very large gentleman was walking down the aisle towards my part of the plane. Did I say very large? I meant horribly huge! Did I say walking? I meant moving, in the way a landslide moves, very deliberately wiping out everything in its path.

It was at this point the voices in my head started to commentate on the unfortunate unfolding events: *'Oh shit, he's gonna sit right next to you. Oh my God he looks grotesque, a male version of that fat lady from Shallow Hal. Why don't you ever get Gwyneth Paltrow sitting next to you?'*

As he got ever closer I started to feel sick in my stomach. And the voices continued: *'You know it, you know it, he's gonna sit RIGHT next to you. YOU are one unlucky bastard.'*

What happened next I considered a minor miracle. There was a voice from the front; I think it was one of the stewardesses. 'Sir, sorry I meant 5a, not 25a.

You're here, near the front'. At this the fat gentleman turned, in a very slow sort of way and acknowledged the lady in the blue suit. He then made a 180 degree turnaround and made his way back towards the front of the plane.

I couldn't contain my relief any longer. As I stared at the number above my seat, the number 25b, I uttered the words, 'thank fuck for that!'

Now and again the voices in my head actually vocalise. They can get me into all sorts of trouble.

A smart looking lady in a white blouse sat just in front of me turned her head to give me a terribly dirty look. The guy in the seat behind sniggered and said, 'you're not wrong there mate, what a bloater!'

I raised my eyebrows in agreement, smiled and turned to face the front of the plane. I then decided I'd better keep my head down for a while.

Just over an hour later my favourite part of the journey arrived, it was the time they feed you. I had booked the in-flight meal and as ever was looking forward to trying to attain the required level of dexterity in order to successfully consume my meal. It was like trying to do a normally simple task like walking, but with your shoelaces tied together. It was almost impossible, like talking sense after ten pints of Stella.

Trying to eat an in-flight meal required being able to operate plastic eating utensils in very tightly confined spaces. It required great skill and top notch hand to mouth coordination. However, having once been accused of being able to peel an orange one handed in my pocket I was ready for the challenge.

These in-flight meals were not particularly filling, which could be the understatement of all time, but in my experience the mix of a small bread roll, butter, savoury biscuits, soft cheese, a hot main course, a dessert and all the necessary condiments was incredibly fun to eat. This for me was a meal I enjoyed and today was no exception. However, the main course being described as *Bangers and Mash* was stretching it somewhat. At one point I imagined the Trade Descriptions Team giving the airline in question a red card for the fact they'd given two cocktail sausages, seven peas and a teaspoon of mashed potato this very misleading description. It had to be said it was an extremely small portion; in fact the name itself was just about bigger than the dish! Nonetheless, in defence of the airline caterers it tasted half decent and I gobbled it down.

The rest of plane journey was relatively eventless. I watched a couple of films. The plane had those little TV's that drop down from the ceiling. The picture was pretty naff, but it killed a few hours.

The landing was smooth and when we started to decelerate on the runway the holiday makers started to applaud the efforts of the pilot. I of course joined in, I am British after all. We gave him a rapturous round of applause and all because he didn't kill us. We were an appreciative crowd!

Chapter Four

On arrival I gathered my case and headed out of the airport for more instructions. A lady waving a Thomas Cook flag saw me looking in her direction. 'Thomas Cook?' she enquired.

I was tempted to say: *'No, Ed Crawshaw'*, but managed to restrain myself.

'Yes, I'm going to Protaras.' I said.

'Coach number one, just follow the crowd, I'll be there shortly.'

I found the coach, found a seat and relaxed. About ten minutes passed by before the lady from Thomas Cook climbed onto the coach.

'Welcome to Cyprus, my name's Tina.' she announced. Then she continued to give us her well rehearsed spiel. 'It'll take us forty five minutes to Ayia Napa and a further twenty minutes to Protaras.' I cursed under my breath. It had already been a long day.

We eventually arrived at Protaras and the Andreotis Hotel. I grabbed my case and walked into the hotel reception. A local man took my passport and handed over a key. I found my room, quickly unpacked my case and headed for the bar. I needed a beer or three.

I met George and his brother Tasos who ran the bar and they made me feel at home and as I started to relax I began to appreciate what I'd been told by numerous people when I talked about my impending holiday. They had all said that the Cypriots were lovely people. They were right.

The two Cypriot brothers were aided and abetted by two European beauties, the dark and mysterious Helena from Moldova and Yvonne, a blonde haired lovely from Ayrshire, her broad Scottish brogue cutting through every other accent in the bar like a sharp knife. I happened to mention to Helena that I was writing a book and suddenly she looked interested.

'You are writer?' she said with a slightly overcooked Russian twang. 'You are so clever.'

She obviously associated writers with being both very clever and very rich. Apart from the former **and** the latter I couldn't argue with her.

After a few more beers I decided to call it a night. If I was to get the most out of this holiday I needed to be on top of my game. After all I was going to write a book. The trouble was I hadn't a clue what this book was to be about. I realised I was seriously *missing a plot*.

The next morning I awoke with a purpose. This was to be the day when I started to put pen to paper or more accurately finger, and note the singular and not the plural, to keyboard.

I got up and had a bit of breakfast to start the day. My usual was a combination of various cereals, normally at least three types, with a finely chopped banana.

Being on holiday I settled for Kellogg's Fruit and Fibre, this was obviously just a single cereal, rather than a combination of several, but gave the impression that several elements were involved! *Anal* or *what*!

Needless to say I of course included my customary chopped banana. It was designed to set me up for the day. It seemed to do the job and I felt good.

Half way through the morning I decided to let the outside world into my room and proceeded to open all the curtains and blinds. I then put the kettle on and had a coffee. I had packed just enough instant coffee for the trip in a small Tupperware style container. I know I have annoyed several people over the years with my seemingly obsessive precise forward planning, and of course I mean women! Men do this sort of thing. It's not a character flaw; it's quite normal male behaviour. Most women seem to run a mile from the type of man that obsessively plan ahead in this way;

'Why can't you be more spontaneous?' Or something like that is the usual cutting remark uttered.

I think that this type of practical pre-planning behaviour reminds women of their elderly fathers. Don't they say that most women are looking for a man like their father?

Yes, as long as he doesn't pack just enough coffee for two people for a seven day break in an ideally sized plastic container. That's just a little ***too much*** like your father!

However, when their man fails to deliver on a simple task like providing an early morning cup of coffee they are the first to stick the knife in. Trust me you just can't win.

Anyway after coffee I started to get that feeling that you get and I knew that a certain call of nature was moments away, for those that are hard of thinking I needed the sitting down version! I'll obviously not go into great detail in order to keep the sensitive ones among us on board, but needless to say as usual my movement was swift and the task was soon completed!

As they say when in Rome do as the Romans do. Well I was in Cyprus and I had to follow suit with Cypriot toilet behaviour and the tissue was duly deposited into the bin provided.

However, being the very hygienic man that I am I decided to use the adjacent sink as a bidet. I cursed the fact that I hadn't packed any wet wipes and made a mental note to pick some up from the supermarket.

I was doing the necessary bottom cleansing in a most satisfactory way when a feeling of slight uneasiness came over me.

It was at that moment that I turned and in a split second saw a shadow move across my peripheral vision. In a heartbeat I realised my plight, earlier I had opened the curtains and blinds and I was now in full view of the balcony of one of my neighbours. One or a number of holiday makers in the Andreotis Hotel had just witnessed me washing my bum! I quickly reacted and closed the toilet door. I then slowly and quite nervously opened it a few centimetres to check whether my audience was still on the balcony. Fortunately whoever was there had gone.

Then to my horror a young man, obviously the principal witness to the crime, was dragging his girlfriend onto their balcony and pointing in my direction. I closed the door and decided to stay in the toilet and out of sight for some time.

Some twenty five minutes later I opened the toilet door very tentatively to check that the coast was clear. I was pleased to see that the overlooking balcony was now empty. I'm guessing the girlfriend was disbelieving of what her boyfriend had apparently seen or had got seriously bored with waiting for the strange man in the toilet opposite to show his face. From my point of view I was hoping that my face wasn't actually seen, although it had to be said there was little doubt that my bottom had been seen in all its glory.

It wasn't the start to the day I had been planning and I certainly learned a valuable lesson. When washing your arse, check you're doing it in private!

The book I was supposedly writing was not even on the radar. The total embarrassment of the morning was the only thing on my mind. Would I ever finish my book? I quickly realised that more importantly at this stage, the question should be would I ever start it?

Chapter Five

It was time to get serious; I had to find a plot-line. I'd already decided that the book was about a man who goes away to write a book, but he can't find the plot. The idea was all well and good, but it was miles away from a finished book.

In search of inspiration I considered some of the book ideas I'd already had in my life. Previously I had started a short story about a group of children that were being haunted by a malevolent supernatural being I had called *Shadows*.

I hoped one day to finish this story, but I knew that it was a totally different genre to my current idea. I also considered another short story I had written when I was in my early twenties about bullying. This story was entitled, *A is for Apple, B is for Bully*. However, again I soon realised the same applied to this short story. It was a book for children and that's all it would ever be. I needed a fully grown up plot for a fully grown up book.

Don't they say that you should write about what you know? I started to trawl through the annuls of *my life* and the various *interesting* experiences I have had along the way.

It was to be a journey that made me cringe.

The first port of call was my time at a local hosiery factory in Sutton-in-Ashfield, my home town. I was working in the Building Maintenance Department of the factory. In my case this meant I was an unskilled labourer, having failed to get the A-Level results I was trying to achieve to go onto University. It was the early eighties and I had just met a lady who was to become my wife. The thing was that whilst I wasn't absolutely destitute, I was short of the type of money you needed to impress a woman. In fact I could just about afford to buy her a few drinks. I was at the time still living with my parents and had just bought my first car, a red Morris Marina Coupé.

I remember my Dad saying at the time, 'you'll never have any money now, running a car is bloody expensive.' How right he was. The truth was I didn't have much money anyway, I'd have less now.

I was due to take my girlfriend out for a meal the following night, which was a Friday when a guy I knew pointed out that one of my rear tyres needed replacing.

On closer inspection it appeared that both of the rear tyres and one of the front tyres were in dire need of replacement.

I made several enquiries and discovered it was going to cost about twenty five pounds per tyre. I was in need of a brainwave. I could ask my parents of course, but they were only just making ends meet and I was fiercely independent. Moreover I could also hear my Dad saying those deeply annoying words, 'what did I tell you son? You'll never have any money now!'

No, asking my parents for money was not an option. I needed a plan.

What happened next was absolutely true and to this day I still deeply regret my actions. The other person concerned still doesn't know what I did. I have decided not to name the victim to protect his innocence or more to the point to protect myself from a mouthful of abuse if I see him again, which I do from time to time. I hope one day we'll be able to talk about it and have a laugh together, without him wanting to throttle me!

It was about three o'clock on the Friday afternoon and in my experience was a quiet time of the day. I was parked around the back of the factory right next to my colleagues' car. Of course our close proximity was part of my plan hatched the night before.

At the time of the crime my colleague was busy dealing with a maintenance emergency, I can't remember what exactly. Probably a blocked drain or something and I made out I was busy doing a repair job in our Work Shop.

If you hadn't worked it out yet, my colleague also had a Morris Marina and I was about to swap three of his good tyres for three of my bad ones.

Missing the Plot

There were no scares or incidents as I carried out my act of theft. Within twenty minutes or so in a calculated and methodical way, one by one, I removed his tyres for mine and visa versa.

I often look back and wonder what the hell I would have said if anyone had caught me in the act, never mind, heaven forbid the owner of the car in question. Owned by a man I actually considered a friend. The mind boggles!

Well I had got away with it and now was the proud owner of three perfectly good tyres and my date with the future Mrs Crawshaw was still on.

The following Monday morning I reported back to work and we had our customary cup of tea and our *"what did you do at the weekend"* chat. I waxed lyrical about how well my date had gone on the Friday night and the fact that we had seen each other on the Sunday as well and my colleague moaned about having to spend nearly a hundred quid on four new tyres.

'Wow, four new tyres!' I said, 'what a bummer!'

I then realised I had taken his three perfectly good tyres and left him with his one bad tyre and of course the three incredibly dodgy tyres that once belonged to me.

I have never done anything like this before or since. I believe I am a changed man now. At the time I was incredibly irresponsible and seemingly without any scruples. I was guilty of committing a potentially dangerous act, and most regrettably it was also towards a so called friend. I was a cad of the lowest order and I apologise profusely. I am seriously relieved that nothing untoward happened as a result of my madness, although it has to be said the hundred pounds I saved came in very handy!

On second thoughts forget protecting the innocent, I ought to make a proper apology to my old friend. Here goes…. I'm sorry Brian!

My second port of call was to a slightly earlier time at the same Hosiery factory. In fact the reason I was there in the first place was the fact that I'd met a young lady who was the daughter of the Manager of the Building Maintenance Department. At the time I was out of work and he offered me a temporary job for a couple of weeks in the summer of 1982. I of course accepted.

Soon after I was invited for Sunday tea and once again accepted.

The meal was typical 1980's Sunday tea fodder, with salmon sandwiches, various salad dishes and new potatoes followed by mandarin orange flan with evaporated milk. Sheer heaven!

Afterwards my girlfriend and I retired to her room to play some music, and to undertake a bit of snogging of course!

It was around this time when I realised that my bowels were beginning to stir a little. You may be noticing a pattern emerging here! Not one of my more endearing features!

I enquired where I could find the loo and was given the necessary instructions to find it. 'Upstairs, second door on the right.'

With moments to spare I sat down and grabbed a nearby magazine to keep me occupied for a moment or two. It has to be said my bowels were noted for their regularity.

One of my favourite quips is the one that goes: 'Yes I'm very regular; I have a number two every morning at 7.30 on the dot. The trouble is I don't get up 'til 7.45.'

Believe it or not I've got many a laugh over the years with that old joke and it has to be said many a groan as well!

Anyway back to the time in my boss's toilet: After I'd done the business I pulled the chain and then I realised that something was terribly wrong. It was one of those times in your life when you want the ground to open up and you would gladly jump into the crevice to hide from the embarrassment.

There it was, the stuff of nightmares, making its way across the poshly tiled bathroom floor on a flood of toilet water. In my mind I could hear the cries of laughter at my predicament from my new workmates and my new boss, who given the situation would probably soon be my new "ex" boss.

Inside my head I was pleading my defence: *'The toilet was blocked. It wasn't my fault. The toilet was blocked!'*

I could almost see the look of sheer disbelief on my soon to be ex-girlfriends face at the horrendous situation that was unfolding in the bathroom of her parents plush superior detached dormer bungalow. The dormer bungalow might have been superior, but trust me the toilet was distinctly inferior!

At this point there was a light tapping on the bathroom door. I guess I'd been gone for a little too long and obviously my girlfriend had stepped upstairs to enquire how and what the hell I was doing.

'I'll be with you shortly.' I said nervously.

'Are you sure you're okay in there?' She sounded concerned.

'Yeah I'm fine; a slight problem, but all sorted now. I'll be out in a minute.'

What happened next is the stuff of legend and will certainly live with me until I die. I managed to clean up the debris from the floor and mop up the water. I repaired the toilet and composed myself. My only problem now was the offending item that had sadly refused to disappear down the pan. I had decided not to try and send it on its merry way down the toilet bowl, just in case the same thing happened again.

Another plan was hatched. I carefully wrapped the thing in loads of toilet paper and held it very lightly, just in case of any further mishap.

It's not something you do everyday. I hope! It felt thoroughly weird and completely surreal.

I then slowly opened the bathroom door and checked that the coast was clear, fortunately for me it was. I made my way down the stairs and along the hallway to the front door with the *"pooh parcel"* tucked safely behind my back.

I very quietly opened the front door to the bungalow and slowly tiptoed around the back of the property where I hoped to find a dustbin in order to deposit the problem package. Not for the first time today!

As I passed by my girlfriend's window I'll never forget the knowing look in her eyes and total humiliation I was feeling at the time.

We laughed for some time when I later explained the events to her. I don't think she ever looked at me in the same light again and we were doomed as a couple.

You don't block your girlfriends parents' toilet and then carry the contents around like your taking part in some warped SOS training manoeuvre and continue to have the same relationship as before.

The events were both hilarious and totally embarrassing and as I look back in years to come it's likely to be one of the most memorable moments of my life.

Soon after we parted and I often wonder what happened to her. Whatever it was she ended up doing

Paul Chadbourne

I'm sure she'll never forget our fleeting time together, if only for my antics in the toilet department.

I hope you're well Jane.

Chapter Six

Back in present day Cyprus I had decided that my yester-year exploits were probably too embarrassing and guilt ridden to be included in my book. And anyway I don't want total strangers reading about these things. After all it's personal stuff!

With that I smiled to myself as the image of me in my late teens carrying my own tissue-wrapped *number two* finally exited my minds eye.

It was a bright sunny new day in Protaras and I had a good feeling. I was sure that my missing plot was just around the corner.

I decided to call home and bought a phone card for ten euros. First of all I decided to call my parents. Dad answered.

'Hi Dad, its Ed from Cyprus.' I said with bags of enthusiasm. Dad replied in his usual manner, 'I'll get your Mum.'

In Cyprus I was shaking my head when Mum came on the phone. Her phone skills were much more advanced than Dads and we talked for several minutes. I told her what a great time I was having. She seemed impressed that I was talking to her from half way around the world and I guess it is quite impressive when you think about it. She wished me well and I ended the call. I decided I would try to get hold of Tony at his office in Mansfield.

The phone rang several times and Tony answered very professionally.

'Tone it's me mate, Ed.'

Instantly his professionalism went out of the window and we were exchanging insults in various silly voices as we'd always done.

'Anyway, how's the book going?'

'Not so good Tone, I was going to include some dodgy exploits from my past, but thought better of it.'

'For Christ's sake don't put the one about the tyres in. If he ever reads it, he'll have you.'

'I don't think there's much chance of anyone reading it Tone, its a million miles away from being written.'

'You'll get there mate. Lena Martell!'

And with that he burst into Lena Martell's massive number one song from the late 70's: *'One day at a time sweet Jesus. That's all I'm asking of you. Lord help me today, show me the way, one day at a time.'*

His version didn't have Lena's grace and tuning, but it did the trick for me.

On the other end of the line in Cyprus I was smiling. I thanked him from the heart and said I had to go to catch a few rays of the Cyprus sunshine and maybe even do some work on the book.

'See you soon mate.' I said. And with that I hung up and headed to the supermarket to pick up some supplies.

By the time I got back to the hotel any thoughts about writing some of the book had faded and despite my feeling of enthusiasm I was resigned to the fact that today would be a day for thinking and very little doing.

I searched for some motivation, but never found it. I only found a pleasant sort of lifestyle with a nice long walk along the beach near Fig Tree Bay and a dip in the hotel pool between a light lunch and reading *the ex-boyfriends handbook* by Matt Dunn. I'm a fan of his.

I walked by the hotel bar and noticed a sign for that night's entertainment. Later that night the hotel was having a quiz night and bingo. Whilst I'm not a bingo follower, I do enjoy taking part in the odd quiz. I smiled to myself and decided that I would definitely be taking part. It would be a chance to meet some new friends and maybe even get some material for the book. Maybe it would be the inspiration I was looking for?

The day passed very gently with more reading, more swimming, and a little bit of snoozing. As the sun began to cool a little I headed back to the room and had a cup of coffee and watched a bit of TV. Looking in the mirror I noticed I'd caught the sun a little and made a mental note to take a little more care the following day, and actually use the sun cream I'd brought with me. After all I didn't want to get burnt.

I needed a shave and shower and after a quick change of clothes I was ready for action.

Some twenty five minutes later I arrived at the bar and grabbed a table for one next to four very loud women of various ages. They were taking digital photos of each other and I boldly interrupted them to suggest I take one of the four of them. They agreed that it was a good idea and I proceeded to take a couple of photos and then handed back their camera. I turned back to my table for one. I felt quite content when I heard the sounds of satisfaction as they admired my work. It's nice to hear that sound.

The quiz started and we were handed a quiz sheet to fill in. They called their team the *Cockney Four*. They were from London. I cheekily suggested the *Cockney Rebels*. Was I being a bit too forward?

I called my team, which was just me, *Solitaire*. I'd given the name some serious thought. I had considered *One Sad Git* and *Billy No Mates* but quickly dismissed them as soon as they entered my head.

The prizes for the winners and runners up were announced. The winning team would receive a bottle of vodka and the runners up a bottle of red wine.

The quiz was about to start and I decided to have some fun with the Cockney girls. They looked like they were up for a good time and a good laugh. Sue was the mum, on holiday with her daughter Louise and niece Katherine. The quartet was made up by Cecilia, who was Sue's mum; she preferred to be called "Siss" for short.

In a nutshell the night went like this; I suggested we pool our resources. The two younger girls seemed to be more competitive and wanted to keep their answers a secret.

As more and more of the questions came out I was feeling pretty confident that I was going to do well.

'Which club did Alan Shearer start his professional career?' For me that was no problem. I'd followed his career closely.

'What was the name of Steptoe and Sons horse?' Strangely I knew that one too.

'Which club did Alex Ferguson leave to join Manchester United?' A doddle for a true United fan.

'What did the "F" stand for in JFK?' I managed to dig this particular answer out from the trivial depths of my brain. I'd obviously heard it before and the information had somehow stuck. I couldn't help thinking that it was a pity that my A-Level Biology and Sociology revision hadn't stuck has much as the amount of trivia I'd absorbed over the years. More questions came and I knew most of the answers. I gladly shared them with the girls. I guess that in a way I was showing off a bit.

In fact I reckon I gave the Cockney Four at least eight answers they didn't have a clue about and had actually guessed incorrectly. The end result was inevitable, *Solitaire* (me!) came equal third and the *Cockney Four* won the main prize by one point.

The irony was the East End ladies had actually known some of the answers that had eluded me. 'What was the Vicar of Dibley's characters actual name in the comedy series?' Also, 'what colour was Julia Robert's wig when she first met Richard Gere in Pretty Woman?' Plus several more of the type of questions mainly aimed at, dare I say it, *girls*!

Afterwards I thought to myself, I don't know about being called the *Cockney Four*, the girls were more like the *Crafty Cockneys*!

I have to say they were very magnanimous in victory and offered me a tot or two of their vodka. I declined, but felt pretty happy that I was instrumental in their win. In fact without doubt their victory was partly mine.

Following the presentation of the main prize I had some further amusement with the victors. Siss informed me that Sue, her daughter was one of twins and that her other three children were triplets.

'Wow' I said, 'did you have any single kids?'

'No.' she said cheekily, 'I only did it twice.' We all laughed.

Sue, her daughter went on to say, 'every time mum had sex she had at least two children.'

'It's enough to put anyone off.' I remarked, said with my tongue firmly in my cheek.

We chatted for a while longer and couldn't help but mention the book. They all seemed quite excited and even impressed at the thought that they'd met a budding author. I must admit I enjoyed the moment.

I declined to play the bingo and decided to wander down the main street in Protaras to check out the night-life. A couple of ladies were trying to coax passers by into the Rooftop Bar. Apparently that night the toast of the island was singing. His name was Neal Ross and the leaflet read: Entertainment Cyprus is calling him the male vocalist of the year. Below this statement it said: "He will blow you away".

'How much does he charge for that then?' I joked.

One of the ladies stared at me in a very vacant way, the other burst out laughing. It's good to find a like minded sense of humour now and then.

Mr Ross wasn't all he's was cracked up to be and I decided to head back to the hotel.

I ordered a Black Russian and proceeded to have a game of pool on my own. I had a couple of games and though I say so myself I played like a pro. After

I'd potted the final black George from behind the bar asked in a playful manner, 'had I won?'

'George, I think I came second.' I announced.

He laughed and a guy sitting close by said, 'good answer mate, I've been coming second all day.' His girlfriend smiled.

I couldn't help saying with a hint of a double entendre, 'well, coming second isn't always a bad thing!' He laughed, she blushed and I left to go to bed.

Chapter Seven

It felt like my holiday was going too quickly; I hadn't even started the book. I'd not even begun to settle on a plot line. I once again searched my mind for inspiration. Could I write a bit of a holiday thriller? I quickly abandoned the idea as ludicrous, it just wasn't me.

Then I remembered that at the welcome meeting on the first morning, the rep had said that Cyprus was known as the "island of love".

That was it, inspiration at last. I would try to write a love story or more to the point a romantic comedy.

I was settled on the idea and I just needed to relax for a while to ponder how the plot would unfold. I decided to have a bit of a tanning session around the pool.

It was around midday and pretty hot so I proceeded to apply some Factor 15.

I'd already caught the sun and was determined not to turn into the holiday lobster we see all too often when the Brits are abroad. To avoid any possible embarrassment I decided to apply the sun cream in the privacy of my room.

My arms, legs, front and face were straightforward of course; my back was an altogether different proposition. Maybe this is why we need a partner I thought, someone to rub the sun cream onto your back. It all made sense and I suddenly felt lonely and helpless.

I could of course ask someone to do the unreachable areas for me. But can you imagine the dilemma of which stranger to ask?

Ask a pretty, young lady and she thinks it's a chat up line.

Ask an elderly lady and everyone thinks you're desperate.

Ask a young man and everyone thinks you're gay.

Ask a child and everyone thinks you're a paedophile.

Ask the lady behind reception and everyone thinks you're a sad lonely git.

Ask the man behind reception and everyone thinks you're a sad lonely gay git.

You get the idea……. It's not easy.

I decided to devise my own method of application. I carefully soaked a towel in sun cream and held the towel in both hands behind my back and gently rubbed the lotion in, using the same method you use to dry your back. In a variation on the technique, I was creaming mine instead. I checked in the mirror and was quite happy with the result. I was ready for the sunshine.

I found a suitable sun bed and aimed it in direction of the sun to guarantee an even tan along my body and I lay down on my towel to take in the midday rays.

After about 10 minutes I started to get bored and decided that I would read a little of the Matt Dunn book I was enjoying. I suddenly realised the book was back in my room and in leaning over to grab my hotel room keys the shift in weight resulted in the sun bed tipping up. I didn't so much fall off; it was more of a slide down as the base of the sun bed shot skyward. Of course I made quite a commotion and several pairs of eyes turned to me. I blushed and cursed under my breath. The voices started: *'What a pillock…Try to look cool, for once in your life.'*

At that moment I noticed a pretty young lady sitting over the opposite side of the pool. She had glanced over in my direction and was smiling at my mishap. She was reading one of Matt Dunn's earlier books, *The Best Man*.

I found myself thinking that this could be a sign. Who was I kidding; tens of thousands of women have probably read it.

The other sun beds and assorted stuff untidily lying around her suggested there were at least two other people in her party, but these people were obviously in the pool or elsewhere. *'Husband and child.'* I thought to myself. *'They're probably playing in the pool.'*

I quickly scanned the area and saw two young children playing in the shallow end. I thought no more about it and accepted that a pretty lady like that would definitely be with someone.

Still we already had one thing in common; we both enjoyed reading books from a certain author.

In all the commotion and subsequent embarrassment I had forgotten about the book I was going to read. I still needed to go and retrieve it from my room.

On the way back to my sun spot I noticed a one euro coin immediately adjacent to the pool side. No-one appeared to be around and I methodically did what I'd done many times in my life. I casually bent down to tie my shoelace. I craftily placed my shoe over the coin, hiding it from view and continued to undo then re-tie my lace. I then quickly palmed the coin and started to stand, a wonderfully perfected *hand is quicker than the eye* manoeuvre based on years of training.

It was at this moment when two things happened simultaneously. First of all a small girl bumped into me from behind just as I was at a vulnerable point in my stance and a small boy came out of the pool directly in front of me.

He was shouting at me in an accent I recognised: 'Hey mister, that's mine.'

I was startled by the sudden appearance of the boy and his deafening cry, and I was instantly filled with guilt. This along with the bump from behind caused me to lose my balance and to topple into the freezing water, along with my copy of *the ex-boyfriends handbook*.

The suddenness of the dunking caused me to swallow some of the pool water and I coughed and spluttered in an attempt to clear it from my mouth and throat. I was slowly catching my breath; though certainly any crumb of dignity was disappearing rapidly. I somehow managed to prevent the book from getting too drenched, although it was a little damp in places.

I gingerly made my way to the safety of the poolside. I noticed that the boy had pulled himself out and was stood beside the young girl.

At that moment a lady who must have been their mother appeared.

'What's wrong Mattie?' she said with a broad Yorkshire accent.

'That man's nicked my money.' the boy said. He was pointing at me.

I awkwardly scrambled out of the water, shook myself down and wiped the water from my face. 'Hiya.' I said with a hint of nervousness. 'You must think I'm a right buffoon!' She didn't appear to argue and my attempt at humour fell on deaf ears as she had other more pressing matters to deal with.

Missing the Plot

'Have you got my sons' money?'

'Well I found a one euro coin on the side, but it didn't have his name on it.' I replied a little too sarcastically.

'Well it's his! So I suggest you hand it back.'

It was then that I realised I no longer had the coin. It had fallen from my grasp as I'd fallen into the water.

'I hate to tell you, but I must have dropped it.'

I began to stare at the approximate place where I'd fallen into the water. After a moment of careful concentration I spotted what I was looking for. With a deep hint of sarcasm aimed at the boy and his mother, I pointed towards the shiny circular object on the bottom of the pool and in my best pirate voice said, 'there's your treasure Jim lad!'

The mother tutted and shook her head in embarrassment and without further adieu the boy dived back into the water to retrieve his money.

It was then I realised that the lady in front of me was the very same lady I had spotted earlier, the one with the similar reading habits.

'Hi, sorry about that, I feel such a fool.' I said, trying desperately to recover some ground.

'Do you make a habit of falling over?' she said with a hint of a smile in her voice. I remembered my earlier mishap and reddened slightly.

'Not usually, it's just been an off-day today.'

Paul Chadbourne

'Anyway, no harm done I guess, apart from your pride.' Again she was smiling as she spoke. It was a nice smile.

A voice from within said: *'This is your way in.'*

'Hey I couldn't help noticing what you're reading. Are you enjoying it? I'm reading his latest.' I was desperately trying to encourage some conversation based on our common literary interests.

She seemed slightly distracted by her daughter. All of a sudden there was a loud blast of Yorkshire in the air. 'LUCY, DON'T DO THAT!'

I turned to see the young girl pouring some water out of a small red bucket onto another child's head.

'They're only playing.' I said, trying to calm her down.

The mother turned to me and glared. Her lips tightened and the expression on her face instantly changed making her nose curl up slightly. She looked me squarely in the eyes and said through gritted teeth, 'when I want your advice I'll ask for it!'

The intense look in her eyes told me she was in no mood to talk any further on the matter.

'Point taken.' I offered in defeat. 'Enjoy the rest of the day.'

In my head I heard: *'Yeah and the rest of your holiday, and the rest of your life!'*

I decided to retreat and leave them to it, knowing when I was beaten. This lady looked as if she could seriously look after herself. She looked pretty well stressed, but I had to admit she also looked **very pretty**.

That night I decided to eat at the Olympus Restaurant which a number of people had recommended to me.

I was dealt with personally by the owner's son who was called Andreas. He recommended a lamb dish that was absolutely delicious. In fact without doubt the best Lamb dish I'd ever tasted, and after the meal that's exactly what I told him. He thanked me and offered to buy me a drink on the house. 'Please Andreas, let me buy you one. I'm Ed, by the way.' With that I smiled warmly and extended my hand towards his.

He gladly shook me by the hand but he declined my offer. 'You come again Mister Ed and you can buy me a drink.'

I agreed that I would and ordered an Irish coffee to make him happy. It was the perfect end to a perfect meal.

I promised him I would return again before I went home and we shook hands again like old friends. I meant it.

I have to say the hospitality at the Olympus was second to none. If the Cypriots could bottle this hospitality they would all be millionaires. However, I got the distinct impression that if they could bottle the feeling of a satisfied customer and good feedback on the meal that would do them fine. The Cypriots are up there with the best hosts in the world. Of that I'm sure.

Later that night I had an enjoyable experience with a lovely couple from Bradford, who were staying in the same hotel complex as me. I was enjoying another evening in the Rooftop Bar with a very passable vocalist who was singing loads of swing songs. There was lots of cheeky humour that suited me down to the ground and when Sandie and Keith arrived and sat next to me the night improved even more. Sandie's surname was Shaw and she waxed lyrical about the times in her youth when her name was responsible for getting her all sorts of attention and funny looks from pop fans uncertain whether she was *thee* Sandie Shaw! Keith was an AC/DC fan and a man I really liked, in fact they were both very nice people. Keith kindly bought me a drink and I promised to return the favour given half a chance at some point later in the week. I wasn't able to return the favour at that moment. As ever I'd taken out a precise number of euros for the evening and typically I was at the point in the evening that I was running out of cash. I needed to cash in a travellers cheque or two. I drank up and bade them farewell and headed back to the hotel.

During the short walk back I was thinking of two completely different things. I didn't know it at the time but they were related in a strange way. The first was that I still hadn't got very far with my Romantic Comedy plot idea; the second was I wonder how the little Yorkshire lady was getting on.

Chapter Eight

The next day I was adamant I was going to start my story. I was almost halfway through my holiday and needed to get a move on. I awoke quite late for me, had my usual breakfast and promised myself that today was the day for Romance. I of course meant the start of the book. Why would I mean anything else?

My first port of call was reception as I needed to cash in some of my Travellers Cheques. I was gathering my notes and coins off the counter when I heard the stomping of feet approaching. I turned to see the Yorkshire lady with her two children in tow getting ever closer. I smiled one of those pleasant little smiles were your mouth stays firmly shut. I remembered our final encounter yesterday and decided that baring a toothy grin was going a little over the top.

I grabbed a leaflet on the Water Park, a local tourist attraction near Ayia Napa, and began to study it in detail. The lady was complaining about something in her room, one of the electric hobs wasn't working too well. The young girl, Lucy, was crawling under some table and chairs and the boy was looking at my leaflet of the Water Park.

'Mum, can we go there?' he said pointing at the leaflet. 'It looks cool.'

'Mattie, how can I take Lucy and you there? You know what she's like; I've all on keeping an eye on you both around the pool.'

The boy pulled a face. His eyebrows straightened and his bottom lip visibly dropped.

I knew I would regret the following interruption. 'Hey if you want some help, I wouldn't mind tagging along.'

She turned slowly to look at me and shook her head from side to side.

'Thanks for the offer, but I'd find it hard enough looking after two children, never mind three.'

I blushed a very deep red and pulled one of those silly faces you pull when you shrug your shoulders. I think it only served to make her point even more. In her mind I was nothing more than a potential burden to her. Not someone to share the load, more like someone to make it much heavier.

'Look it's up to you. I can stay on my feet most of the time and I'm pretty good with kids.' I offered as a comforting thought.

'When you're not stealing their money you mean.'

Then the boy piped up, 'mum why can't we go with him? He seems nice.'

'Just because Mattie, that's why!' There was a degree of finality in her tone.

I caught the boy's eye and we both looked confused at his mother's logic. It was a moment that men share every single day. *Mankind* would never come anywhere close to understanding the female logic.

I instantly warmed to the boy. He was a pretty switched on young man I thought and well advanced in *"man"* thinking for a boy his age.

At that moment Lucy ran towards us and jumped up into my arms.

'Hello.' she said sweetly, 'what's your name?'

'My name's Ed. You're Lucy if I'm not mistaken.'

'Ed.' she said and she repeated the name several times.

I turned to the lady and said, 'well you know my name. Put me out of my misery then. You are?'

'Teri.' she replied. 'It seems the kids' approve.' she added.

I looked down at Lucy who was pulling my sunglasses off the top of my head and then turned to the boy who was smiling up at me with puppy dog eyes. 'It seems so.' I said.

'They maybe feel like you're one of them.'

'I assure you I'm not.' I retorted, a little too quickly even for my own liking.

'A KID I mean!' She emphasised the word to make her point. Point taken.

Missing the Plot

I was going to say it's a pity their mum doesn't feel the same when Teri said, 'It's a pity their mum doesn't feel the same way.'

One of the voices in my head said: *'It's a sign.'*

'Look, what have you got to lose? You can obviously look after yourself. I assure you I'm a nice guy.'

'I don't know any nice guys.'

I believed her. There was a look in her eyes that told me she totally believed it herself.

'Well maybe you don't know it yet, but you've just met one.' I said as I offered my hand to shake hers.

'It's nice to meet you Teri.' She gently took hold of my hand and smiled.

After a few minutes pondering it was decided we would go to the Water Park the very next day.

Later that morning I popped back to the pool to find Teri chatting to a couple by the poolside. I acknowledged her and she gestured me towards them.

I half recognised the couple but couldn't quite place them.

'Ed, this is Rob and Claire, Rob and Claire this is Ed.' she said efficiently.

I smiled warmly. 'Nice to meet you both.' I extended my hand. Rob turned towards his girlfriend and made a strange face with wide eyes. My hand was still held out but Rob made no attempt to take it.

It was then that I recognised them both. They were the couple from earlier in the week, from the balcony opposite. Not for the first time this week I blushed. I could sense they knew it was a knowing blush. I now understood why Rob was so reluctant to take my hand. He knew what I'd been doing with it!

'Very nice to meet you both.' I lied. 'Teri, it's always a pleasure. You must excuse me, I've off down to the beach for a walk.'

'Oh, the kids and I will come if you don't mind. They're bored stiff here.' 'Yeah, fine. I'll meet you in reception in ten minutes?' Anything to escape the now childish sniggers coming from my two neighbours.

'Can you make it fifteen?' she asked and I agreed.

Thirty minutes later they arrived. I was doing my usual pacing around routine. Another habit inherited from my Dad.

'Don't let me interrupt your pacing Ed.' Teri said with a more than a hint of mischief.

'Shall we go?' I suggested.

'Ooops... No I need Lucy's sun cream. I'll just be a mo.' With that she disappeared back towards their room to fetch the said item.

Five minutes later she returned and finally we left to go for our walk. I was already knackered. I reckon I'd already done a few miles pacing. Thanks Dad.

Missing the Plot

The walk went well and the kids seemed to enjoy it. We bought an ice cream at the shop right near the sea on Fig Tree Bay.

'Nice place, Cyprus, don't you think?' I said in an attempt to make conversation.

'I actually used to live here, but this is the fourth time on holiday, I love it.' she replied.

I heard a familiar voice from within say: *'You've hardly been anywhere.'*

Chapter Nine

We arrived back at the hotel and I wished Teri and the kids a nice evening.

'Why, what are you up to?' Teri enquired.

'Don't ask. I've only booked to go on the Reps night tonight in Ayia Napa. I'm dreading it.'

'You'll be fine, I wish I was going.'

'Me too.' I said and instantly regretted the way it came out. 'I mean, it would be nice to know someone else who's going.'

'I know what you mean, that's okay. Just let your hair down, enjoy it!'

'I'll probably be home by midnight knowing me.' I joked.

'Why do you turn into a pumpkin?'

I couldn't think of a witty reply quickly enough and just decided to smile.

I caught the bus into Ayia Napa at 7.15pm. We had to be in a bar called *Bedrocks* at 8pm. I arrived, you guessed it, early.

I scanned around the bar and noticed two young ladies looking my way. I did my usual turning around

Missing the Plot

to see who was behind me routine and when it was obvious they were looking at me, I plucked up the courage to go over and say hello.

'Hi there.' I said confidently, 'are you on the bar crawl?'

The lady nearest to me was obviously slightly confused. 'I am sorry.' she said in an East European accent, 'we are crawling you say?'

'No, sorry, I meant are you on the Thomas Cook bar crawl tonight?'

The young lady just replied, 'we are from Lithuania.'

They were both very pretty, but there was something on the slightly sinister side to them. I wouldn't find out until later in the night what it was.

We chatted for a while and I told them that I was from the UK, near Nottingham.

'Robin Hood country!' I added. It always worked.

'Ah, yes, Robin Hood.' they said together. They smiled at each other and asked me if they could join the bar crawl.

I suggested they just tagged along. The reps started to make the noises that indicated that the bar crawl was about to begin. I along with about fifty revellers had paid ten euros to be here; my two new friends joined me in the queue and of course didn't pay a cent.

The Lithuanian's were called Nele and Indra. We arrived at the second of the six bars on the crawl and were given a green coloured shot as we entered.

I'm not complaining but to me all the shots tasted the same, the red, the blue and the green all tasted the same, they were far too sweet and juicy with a hint of vodka. *'Give me a bottle of bud any day.'* Even my thoughts were showing their age!

There were people already drunk at this stage. They were mainly girls and had obviously started their nights drinking somewhat earlier than the rest of us. Isn't it strange that girls aren't half as pretty when they're vomiting!

I bought a drink and was horrified to find out that half a lager was an extortionate five euros. I quickly realised that I couldn't really afford to buy my new eastern friends a drink, if I hoped to get the slightest bit tipsy myself, and the thought of getting drunk was way out, I'd run out of money long before that happened. It's not that I'm a big drinker, it was more my distinct lack of cash that would determine a relatively sober night. I was also conscious I needed to save at least twenty euros for the taxi fare home. I didn't know it at the time but being quite sober wasn't such a bad thing.

The two girls started to dance to the music and I decided to join in the merriment. I got the distinct impression that I was surplus to their particular requirements. At one point a young guy started to wiggle his hips to the groove with Indra and instantly

Nele's mood changed. Her face dropped and she quite literally threw a strop on her way to the ladies.

When she arrived back some ten minutes later I was stood alone taking in the sights that Ayia Napa had to offer and Indra was dancing with some other fellow. Nele sidled over to me and said in an over the top sexy Lithuanian accent, 'dance with me.'

I obliged of course, but felt I was part of a game. An English pawn in a game of Russian roulette. A bit of mix of metaphors and slightly incorrect geographically speaking, but hopefully you get my drift.

We moved onto a few more bars and the girls were getting tipsier as the free shots and party games, meaning much more of the free shots were flowing.

I lost the girls in the throng of bodies for a while and was happy to be in my own company.

I felt I was definitely getting too old for this when a certain song came through the speaker system and every other person in the room responded in the same manner by thrusting their arms in the air simultaneously in time to the beat. All I could think about was the relative safety of the bar back at the hotel.

I was relieved to see a couple I had briefly met at the Andreotis Hotel back in Protaras. Andrew and Keryn were from New Zealand and looked to be enjoying the night. They recognised me and we talked for a while, agreeing to share a taxi ride back to Protaras later in the night. I must admit I was reaching that point already. I realised I **was** getting too old for this.

Keryn said in a wonderfully vibrant New Zealand voice, 'just say when you're ready, there's no rush, but we're ready when you are.'

At that moment Nele spotted me and I could see she now had a male friend in tow. They approached and she introduced me to her new friend Igor, also from Lithuania. I shook his hand and smiled. I didn't like the look of him one bit.

Nele went to whisper something in my ear. 'I come home with you tonight, yes?' I looked at her and then at Igor and swallowed hard.

'I don't think so, I'm married, engaged, err seeing someone, sorry.'

She just grabbed my head and before I could protest planted a sloppy, toothy, tongue twister of a kiss right upon my open mouth.

It was horrible and I understood how a rock felt when a limpet just wouldn't let go. My particular limpet was from Lithuania and I have to say I didn't like that *you'll never get rid of me* feeling it gave me. But that seemed to be the least of my problems; Igor was now giving me a very strange look. I imagined his pockets full of knives, guns and various weapons of torture.

He was now starting to look even more like an Eastern European psycho, the type that appears in so many movies today, the one that stabs the innocent character in the back when he's not looking. I looked around in the hope of seeing several alternative targets for Igor, but the only innocent character in the room seemed to be me. I shuddered at the thought. Igor was mean and moody, his eyes were dark and menacing and he scared the shit out of me.

I had to think quickly, I smiled at Igor and made some small talk regarding how his evening was going. His response was a stony silence; he just looked at me through eyes that were dead. I could feel the tension inside me turning to panic but I somehow held my nerve. I suggested that we had a drink and asked them what they wanted. Igor requested a large vodka and Nele nodded the same. I made my way to the bar and noted that Igor was making his way to the gents, probably to stab someone I thought. Nele was in deep conversation with her other Lithuanian mate, Indra and I saw my chance for escape.

I quickly caught the eye of Andrew and Keryn and gestured to the door. Thankfully they nodded and in seconds we were heading towards one of the several taxi ranks in Ayia Napa. I nervously looked around to see that we were not being pursued by the Lithuania Mafia or even worse Nele and Igor.

Fortunately there was a taxi waiting, it was only midnight after all. We jumped in and told the driver our destination. Within seconds we were on our way back to the safety of Protaras.

I chatted with my new antipodean friends and within fifteen minutes we were back at the hotel. I insisted on getting the taxi fare of fifteen euros. It was a very small price to pay for my life.

The only place for me right now was the hotel bar for a large stiff drink.

George remembered my tipple from a previous late night drink and enquired with a degree of confidence in his voice, 'Black Russian Ed?'

I had to smile. 'No thanks, I've gone off them George, I'll have a bottle of Bud please.' I'd had enough of Russians for one night, whatever their colour!

Chapter Ten

All thoughts about the book were left to one side. There would be time to write it later in the holiday. Or so I thought.

Today was the day of the Water Park and I have to say just like a big kid, I was excited at the prospect. Of course there was also another reason that my temperature was rising and my adrenaline was pumping and that was the thought of spending some quality time with Teri.

Yesterday we had agreed to meet in reception at 10am. I arrived at 9.45. Teri and the kids arrived with several more decibels of noise at 10.20. I smiled. She asked if I'd been there long. I lied that I'd just arrived myself.

'Stop hanging around then, let's go. Come on kids.' she announced.

This could be a long day I thought. But I still smiled.

We caught the bus at 10.30 and I decided to pay for us all, just five euros in total. Teri smiled and thanked me.

We arrived some twenty five minutes later and we were all amazed by the sheer scale of the park, it was enormous. The kids' faces lit up and their jaws visibly dropped. I tried to contain my excitement. It's good to look a little cool sometimes.

'Don't look so miserable!' Teri said with a playful hint of sarcasm.

I'm not sure I've mastered this looking *cool* thing. Sometimes when I try to look cool I obviously look completely pissed off. 'I'm just in awe Teri, it looks fab.' I said hopefully recovering some ground.

We smiled at each other.

'Make yourself useful then; here grab these bags and stuff.' She shoved three bags and a heap of towels in my arms. I didn't have a chance to argue, and wouldn't have dared anyway.

The kids ran off and Lucy headed straight for the small pool.

Teri was obviously used to these sudden movements from her daughter and shouted, 'Lucy, don't go too far. Stay close by.'

Lucy turned to face us, placed both hands on her hips, wiggled her bottom and said, 'okay mummy!'

Teri and I set up camp by the small pool and kept an eye on what the kids were getting up to. So far everything was going well.

The sun was getting hotter and there was only one thing for it, my shirt was coming off and I'd work a little on my tan.

'Oh Ed, it looks like you've caught the sun on your back in the last few days. You need to be careful today.'

'I thought it felt a bit sore last night.' I replied pretending to be in slight pain. 'I'm afraid it's one of the downsides to being on holiday alone, nobody to rub cream on your back.'

She looked me up and down and in an instant said, 'I'll rub cream on anyone's back, as long as it's not spotty!' She looked around at my back and said, 'you're okay, not too many spots. I'll do yours if you do mine.'

'Sounds ominous.' I replied. Inside my head the voices were teasing me.

Teri lathered me up and I returned the favour, trying not to be too touchy if that's possible when you're touching someone.

Just at that moment Matthew or *Mattie* as Teri called him arrived wanting a drink. He turned to his mum and asked, 'can Ed take me on the giant slide please?'

I turned to Teri and she shrugged, smiled a smile of approval and off the two of us went, the little kid leading the way and the big kid in tow.

The giant slide was aptly named and we were both out of breath as we reached the top of the steps. Looking down was absolutely daunting for me. I wasn't so much afraid of heights, just scared of falling off them!

Missing the Plot

Mattie took it in his stride and when it was our time to go he challenged me to a race. Being a man of course I accepted. We positioned ourselves at the top of the slide in readiness.

'After three.' Mattie called.

I started to count out loud. 'ONE, TWO....'

After two he was already on his way. I shouted after him but I realised I'd been out-done by the boy and the race was almost certainly already lost. However, I was made of sterner stuff and my wild competitive streak meant I wouldn't give in so easily and I hurled myself off the top of the slide with as much effort as I could muster. Within seconds I started to slow down to a pathetic pace and he was going further and further away from me. It was then that I realised that I was not as streamlined as I used to be, a declaration that could be described as the understatement of the year.

I reached the bottom several seconds behind him and landed with an almighty and quite undistinguished splash in the landing pool. I crawled to the side wiping the water from my eyes to be greeted by Mattie screaming to go again. What's a man to do? In for a penny in for a *pounding*, that's me!

The day went very well. We had a picnic, all had an ice-cream, the kids and I had a water fight and generally we all had a great time. Teri seemed to be pleased for some adult company and for someone to take away some of the pressure by playing with the kids. I'd been a big kid all of my life, I loved it.

The Park was starting to empty and we also started to make a move. We gathered our stuff, and made for the bus stop. Lucy, who had obviously taken a shine to me wanted to be carried. I obliged. Matthew was a little more wary although he was smiling up at me. Teri was smiling too.

Everyone was tired as we arrived back at the hotel around 6pm. I helped them back to their room and thanked them for a wonderful day. I mentioned that I might see them later at the *Cyprus night* the hotel bar was putting on. Teri said they had also booked to go. I suggested we could go together if she liked. I added that I'd appreciate the company. I didn't want to come on too strong. The truth was I would appreciate the company, **her** company.

'That would be very nice Ed; we'll probably get there about 7.45.'

I cheekily yet with some degree of accuracy thought to myself, *'I'll see you at 8.15 then'*. But I actually said the words, 'okay I'll see you then.'

I thought about the book and quickly dismissed the thought, I was knackered.

Cyprus night was held in the hotel bar. George, Tasos and the two regular waitresses were joined by another couple of people. It looked like a complete sell-out and all the tables were taken. Fortunately I had arrived a little earlier and had found a cosy table for four near one of those patio heaters.

I ordered a pint of Keo and sat at the table to take in the atmosphere. There were a few people I had met earlier in the week, the cockney girls were there and I waved at them from across the room. They waved back at me with lots of enthusiasm. They were a good bunch and obviously enjoying their stay no end.

After about ten minutes I was amazed to see the relatively prompt arrival of my three companions and I whistled loudly and waved my arms wildly to get their attention. Teri was obviously slightly embarrassed by my gesturing. She was slowly shaking her head in a *there he goes again* sort of way. They arrived at the table and Teri said, 'I *could* see you; you didn't need to make such a scene. How much have you had to drink?'

I smiled and remarked that I was high on life and hadn't had much to drink at all. She gave me one of those *I don't believe you* looks followed by a playful frown.

'Let's get the night moving Teri, what are you having?'

Teri now seemed to relax a little and she asked for a glass of red wine and suggested lemonade to the kids. They nodded in agreement. I made my way to the crowded bar to sort the liquid refreshment. I decided to order a bottle of Shiraz for us to share.

The bar staff started to put the buffet out and the various aromas coming from the piping hot food was divine.

Teri began to tell me more about herself. She had fallen pregnant with Matthew when she was in her mid twenties. The relationship hadn't worked out although the father was still very much in contact with his son.

A year or so later she met and married a soldier. Lucy was born the following year and they had lived here in Cyprus, where he was posted. Obviously the marriage hadn't worked out and one day the father just upped and left Teri and the kids.

She had no choice but to return back home to Wakefield in West Yorkshire.

She told me about her study, she was taking a Law Degree with the Open University. She explained that she found the study very difficult with two young children to look after. It was only with the help of her family and friends that enabled Teri to find the time to complete her studies.

She asked me about my family, my life, my career, my ambitions, and what I was looking for in life. We talked for several hours. She was bright, witty and extremely good company. The time was 10.20pm and it was obvious the kids were flagging.

'Ed, its getting late, the kids are shattered and I'm a little tired too, I'm gonna call it a night, do you mind?'

'No, of course not. I'll walk you to your room.'

'There's no need for that, it's only about 100 feet away.' She smiled.

Still it felt like the gentlemanly thing to do and I insisted. We walked the hundred or so feet to their room and I wished them all a good night.

'Thank you Ed, for today and for tonight.'

You're welcome Teri, goodnight.' I said with a smile and cheeky wink.

I decided to return to the bar for another drink or two and ended up talking to a couple of Geordie's. The father and son, Brian and Gavin were over in Cyprus for a week with their family and had just attended a wedding on the island. I think it was the wedding of Brian's eldest daughter.

We talked for a while, about football mainly. I teased Gavin, who had a broad Geordie accent about the fact his team was Liverpool. His Dad was a proud Sunderland fan, apparently they're called *Makens*. You learn something every day.

A few moments later it was Gavin's turn to tease me when I revealed my allegiance to Manchester United. How can a Nottinghamshire lad, now living in South Yorkshire support a team in the North West? I was accused of being a glory hunter. Touché Gavin.

After one more drink I decided to call it a night myself. It had been a long tiring day, but I'd certainly enjoyed it no end.

I got back to my room and considered getting out my laptop to start the book. The consideration was as far as I got and instead I switched on the television and watched the end of an episode of Desperate Housewives in English with Greek subtitles. The women in this programme were all stunning looking with wonderfully toned and tanned bodies. They didn't look very desperate to me at all.

Chapter Eleven

The next day Teri and I had arranged to have a quiet day together, with the kids around the hotel pool. Its funny *kids* and *quiet* don't normally mix, but they behaved impeccably.

Unfortunately the same cannot be said of the enormous group of family and friends that had just arrived from the UK. The English abroad eh! Makes you want to learn Spanish or Greek and live up in the mountains somewhere remote. Well it does me.

After a while I could tell that Teri was getting a little uptight with their constant gabble and the rest of the holiday makers were certainly tiring of them too.

The vast majority of the men had large breasts and huge stomachs, which I'm guessing were beer bellies, as it was 11.30 in the morning and they were already getting the lagers in. It had to be said that the mass of man boobs was far outweighing the mass of the female kind. I mentioned to Teri that we ought to go into business making man bras. She laughed.

In an instant my male mammary theory was dead in the water as Teri pointed to two very large ladies with gigantic breasts that easily tipped the boob mass game in favour of womanhood, at least around the poolside at the Andreotis Hotel.

I pointed out that I reckoned it was still nip and tuck or quite possibly *'nipple'* and tuck and we laughed again.

So most of the men had huge beer bellies, had tattoos and were bald. The ironic thing was that apart from the baldness this exactly summed up the appearance of most of the women too.

There were of course the odd exceptions to the rule. There was a guy that looked as though he'd swallowed a brick shit-house. He was obviously a body builder and I'd never seen a darker, deeper tan in my life. His wife was pretty and slim. All in all I considered that she looked slightly out of place without the tattoos and the beer belly!

At that moment a young man from the family of English rabble happened to bump into my leg as he was being chased by his mate. The bump was minor and I acknowledged his hand held up as an apology. However, Teri refused to let it lie and she couldn't help but comment that he should have been more considerate. He just ignored her but I was impressed by her nerve.

'You're wasting your breath.' I whispered, 'these people are from another planet.'

She smiled back at me and simply shrugged her shoulders. As if to make my point the young lad screamed and dived into the kiddies' pool knocking over the two little tots that were happily playing there.

'I see what you mean.' Teri whispered.

'Planet Knob-head!' I whispered back.

We arranged to meet a little later for a drink and a bite to eat in Protaras.

I decided to make the best effort I could with what was still clean in my limited wardrobe. I settled on my best jeans, new light brown leather shoes and a short white cotton shirt. It was probably a little too big on me as I'd lost a little weight and it hung a little loosely. However, it was clean and showed off my tan pretty well I thought.

When Teri turned up with the kids they were all looking dapper. She looked stunning in a short linen dress and tan coloured sandals. I couldn't help thinking that she looked slightly different in her facial features to the way she had earlier. In fact I reckoned there were at least four different faces that she had. It sounds strange, but not in an awful way, it's just that she appeared to look like slightly different people at different times. Don't get me wrong they were all quite beautiful in their own way, but with subtle differences to each other. I remember thinking that it was a lovely thing to have, different faces to fit the different moods you're in.

We headed into Protaras and I suggested we ate at the Olympus. I'd really enjoyed eating there earlier in the week and Teri seemed happy with the suggestion and we made our way to the said restaurant.

Andreas met us at the door and made a big fuss of me.

'Ed my friend, welcome back and who is this lovely lady?'

'Andreas, meet Teri.' I said proudly.

He took her hand and kissed the back whilst saying in a very Greek accent, 'it is my pleasure.'

'This fine fellow is Mattie and this is Lucy.' I said gesturing to the two children in turn. Mattie nodded and smiled and Lucy spotted the various dessert offerings displayed in a glass cabinet and was off like a shot. I gave chase and managed to grab her just before she could stick her fingers into one of the strawberry fools.

Andreas promised that if the children ate all of their dinner he would give them a strawberry fool on the house. Teri of course, never one to miss a trick, couldn't help asking what she could have if she ate all of her dinner.

'You can have anything you like Miss Teri, anything at all, any friend of Mister Ed is a friend of mine.' I immediately thought how funny it sounded and whether Andreas was familiar with the television show about the talking horse. I decided to let it lie. Andreas was a bit of a charmer, but I couldn't help but like him.

We settled down at a cosy table for four and scanned the menu. I already knew what I was having anyway; the slow cooked lamb was so delicious last time that I couldn't resist having it again. Teri decided on a slightly different lamb dish on the basis we could mix and match our meal. *'Nice idea'*, I thought.

The kids had a pizza and lemonade each and we ordered a nice bottle of Shiraz.

We chatted about all sorts of things but particularly the fact that Teri wasn't able to finish her law degree at University and how she was determined to complete the points she needed to finish it off over the next few years. I couldn't help but be impressed by her attitude and her drive.

'I want to do it both for me and to make my parents proud, I always felt like I let them down a bit.' she said.

'I'm sure they'll be very proud of you when you finish it.' I replied and then I offered her more wine.

'Are you trying to get me drunk Mr Ed?' she teased.

'What do you take me for, I'm hurt.' I put my hand on my chest and pulled a face with my bottom lip sticking out. I then said in a slight whisper, 'two more bottles over here Andreas.'

He didn't hear me of course, but Teri smiled and shook her head playfully.

We finished our main courses. My choice was once again quite stunning and Teri's was equally good. The kids got their strawberry fools and Teri and I opted for an Irish whiskey each.

I can honestly say the evening had gone very well and we agreed to split the bill. I thought to myself that this was unusual and a good sign.

Whenever I'd dated a lady in the past I'd usually always pay for meals and stuff, if only to avoid any embarrassment about who *would* or *should* pay. I hated that moment when the bill arrived. I had a reputation of that of a generous gentleman. But many of my mates thought otherwise and they preferred to use the phrase *'gullible git.'*

I reminded myself that this wasn't actually a date and there was no reason why we shouldn't split the bill. But I was still impressed that she'd offered, and of course I accepted her offer, after all I'm an honorary Yorkshire-man nowadays!

The time was getting on and the kids were beginning to get restless so we decided to head back to the hotel. Teri wanted to settle the kids down in her room and relax for the rest of the evening.

'Okay, well I'll walk you back and leave you to it.' I said whilst thinking about what to do myself. Maybe I'd pop to the hotel bar or head into Protaras to a Karaoke bar or something.

'Oh, I thought you might join me for a glass of wine on my balcony when the kids have settled down.' she said invitingly.

'Oh right!' I had both surprise and delight in my voice, 'that sounds great; I'll grab a bottle of Shiraz on the way back to the hotel then.'

Teri smiled and said, 'why don't you make it two bottles?'

It was my turn to smile.

I popped into the nearest supermarket and bought two bottles of Shiraz and a bar of dairy milk, I was partial to a few blocks of chocolate with my wine.

We arrived back at the hotel and I walked them to their room. I said I'd just need to pop back to my room for ten minutes and then I'd come straight over. I quickly freshened up, changed my shirt and sprayed a little more Hugo Boss on my chin and neck. It's good to make an effort, I wasn't expecting anything to happen but I was going to smell pretty good if it did.

I arrived at Teri's room about 15 minutes later.

'I thought you'd got lost.' was her greeting to me.

I bit my tongue and decided not to mention the fact that she had complete double standards on tardiness. She dished out being late all of the time, but couldn't take someone being late in return. It's best to bite your tongue sometimes and I figured it wouldn't have been the best start to the rest of our evening. I just smiled and walked into the room to pour a couple of glasses.

The kids were so tired that they were almost asleep when I arrived. It was now Teri's turn to freshen up and when she announced she would just be a couple of minutes I had to bite my tongue again and I simply said, 'okay.'

You guessed it some 15 minutes later she joined me on the balcony looking more refreshed. I handed her a glass of wine and we began talking.

I told her about my feelings about relationships and that I was an all or nothing sort of guy. 'It's just the way I am Teri, I'm not at all possessive but I have to put everything into whatever I do.'

Teri was obviously carefully considering my words and then quietly said, 'that's okay if you both want the same thing at the same time; otherwise I'm sure it could cause problems.'

'We are what we are Teri and I can't be what I'm not.'

'Fair enough.' she said, 'you're right in one way though; you have to be yourself in a relationship.'

I nodded in agreement and poured her another glass of Shiraz.

We went on to talk about what we were both looking for in life. Teri wanted to carry on with her study and continue to look after her kids and try to give them both the best education, things like that. I told her about the fact that I'd come to Cyprus to write a book. She asked me what it was about.

When I explained I decided it would be a romantic comedy she seemed delighted. 'Oh maybe I'll be in it?' That would be so cool.' she said with excitement. She sounded thrilled at the thought of being in the book and it gave me quite a buzz that the idea of the book excited her so much. But I knew it was far from complete and I was starting to seriously think that I'd never actually finish it. However, I kept my negative thoughts to myself and said that I was planning for her to be in it. At that she beamed one of the most amazing smiles I'd ever seen.

I asked her about settling down. She replied that if she ever found a nice guy she might consider it one day. 'Present company accepted Ed, I know you're nice, but you know what I mean!'

I spoke about my recent separation from Marie and that I wanted to continue with my business interests and eventually find someone to settle down with who had lots of things in common with me.

'I think that doing things together is so important. It's what successful relationships are built on.' I said with conviction.

It was Teri's turn to agree with a nod of her head at the same time she slurped a glug of red wine, almost spilling it. I gently wiped away the drop from the side of her mouth and she thanked me.

We went on to talk about our interests, desires and hopes for the future. There were so many things we wanted that were very similar and I was pleased to hear that Teri was like minded. I opened the second bottle of wine and we continued talking.

'What happened to your marriage Ed? You were together a long time.'

'I don't really know, I guess we just grew apart. The kids moved away and we seemed to drift. Believe it or not it happens a lot.'

There must have been an obvious sadness in my voice because Teri put her hand on my shoulder and said, 'I can see it still hurts a lot.' She then added that line that everyone seemed to say: 'But time is a great healer as they say.'

'So they say, so they say.' I thought for a moment and said, 'but I reckon that basically we move on because we start to forget about the pain. Life just goes on; you have to go with it.'

There were a few moments of awkward silence before Teri spoke again. Her voice was soft and measured and she simply said, 'I suppose so.'

Half an hour later the second bottle was gone and it was getting late and a little cooler. I was getting tired myself and actually yawned loudly.

'Oh, am I keeping you up?'

'No not at all, it's just been a long day. I really ought to get going, thanks for a lovely evening Teri.'

'You're welcome Ed, I've enjoyed it too.'

Then at precisely the same moment we both started to stand. The drink had taken its toll and we were both slightly worse for wear and as I leaned forward in my stance, so did Teri. This only served to cause a coming together of our heads. It wasn't too hard but Teri immediately rubbed her head not knowing whether to smile or wince. Then we each laughed a stifled laugh. It was getting late after all.

'I'm sorry about that Teri, I was going to kiss you goodnight, but I understand that in Wakefield you bang heads instead!'

She smiled, 'I know! It's a strange custom! It takes some getting used to, but you'll get to like it in the end.'

'Oh does that mean we'll get the chance to bang our heads together again then?' I bravely remarked.

'Who knows.' she replied. The wine had taken its toll and both of us were starting to flirt a little. Teri flicked her eyelashes and said, 'perhaps we could try a normal kiss without the head butt one night?'

'Yes, there's doing head and there's *doing head*. I know which I prefer.' I knew I was being very cheeky, but it was clear we both enjoyed the banter.

I leaned forward to peck her on the cheek. At that moment she turned her head to grab the empty glasses off the table and my kiss landed squarely on her lips. I immediately pulled away and apologised. She smiled back at me and asked if I'd prefer a head butt instead.

She was as sharp as a razor and I really liked her sense of humour. I leaned forward again and actually managed to kiss her on the cheek this time.

'Night Teri, perhaps I'll see you tomorrow?'

'If you don't you'll be in big trouble.' she said with a smile. 'Sleep well.'

That night I slept like a proverbial baby, and I don't mean that I was constantly wetting the bed and waking up screaming; on the contrary I went off like

Missing the Plot

a lark and dreamt all night about the lady I'd met in Cyprus. She was from Wakefield in West Yorkshire and she seriously interested me in so many ways.

Chapter Twelve

The very next day I awoke with thoughts of the night before. Had I behaved myself properly, had I offended Teri in any way, why was there a small lump on my forehead and why was it a little sore?

I suddenly remembered our bout of head tennis and smiled to myself. How had I managed to bang heads with this lady? What an impression to make.

I helped myself to some breakfast and turned my thoughts to the book. I was serious about writing it and I felt sure that maybe Teri could be the inspiration I was looking for. I decided that I would talk to her about my plans and maybe even get her advice on how to get the thing started, after all she was a smart cookie!

It was at that moment that there was a tapping noise on my door and I realised that I was in no fit state to answer it without putting on a pair of shorts and a shirt. I donned the necessary clothing and gingerly opened the door to reveal Mattie standing there.

Missing the Plot

'Hello mate.' I said. 'Good morning to you, what are you guys up to?'

Mum sent me to see if you have any aspirin or paracetemol, she's not feeling too well.'

'Okay I see. Let me think, just give me a moment. Do you want to come in?'

'My mum says I shouldn't go into the rooms of strange men.' I felt a little hurt to be labelled as *strange*. Although some would argue it wasn't far off the mark.

'No worries mate, its okay I've found them anyway. Take these back to your mum and ask her if there's anything else she needs?' I handed a couple of paracetemol to Mattie and sent him on his way.

I put the kettle on to make myself a coffee and just at the time it began to boil the tapping at the door returned. I opened the door to find both Mattie and Lucy stood there.

'Hello again.' I said, 'long time no see, how's your mum?'

'She's sent us round to ask you something. She said can you pop and see her for a minute she needs to ask you something important.'

'Okay I'll be with you shortly.' I said.

I hurriedly gathered my things and within a minute or two was ready to go.

We arrived back at Teri's room and I knocked on the door. Seconds later the door opened and I was met by a distinctly rough looking Yorkshire lady.

'Hiya, you look like you've seen better days.'

She just looked at me through squinting eyes and managed a very strained smile. I noted that this was yet another new face for Teri. Certainly one I'd not seen before and definitely not one of her best.

'I'm sorry; it must have been something I ate.'

'Do you think so?' I said with a large dose of irony, 'nothing you drank then?'

Again she squeezed out another strained smile, bent double for a second holding her stomach and made a quick dash for the toilet bowl.

After a few minutes of various strange sounds emitting from the bathroom she re-emerged looking even rougher than before.

'Ed can I ask you a big favour?' she asked.

'Of course, fire away.'

'It's the kids, I don't like to ask, but could you just look after them for a while?' She looked at me through pleading eyes and went on to say, 'it's only for a few hours 'til I get my head **and** stomach in gear.'

'Teri that's fine and I'm actually quite flattered. I'll take them to the pool and we'll just chill out for a while. You get yourself better. Do you need anything? Indigestion tablets, more painkillers, a stomach pump?'

My attempt a humour went right over head. She just stared at me blankly with a very pale expression.

'Thanks Ed, are you sure you don't mind?'

I was beginning to think that this wasn't exactly what I had in mind for today. I smiled as warm a smile as I could manage and said, 'it will be my pleasure dear.'

Within a few minutes the kids and I were making our way towards the pool. It was quite early still; although the sun was already beating down. We found ourselves a suitable spot and laid down the towels and other items to make the spot our own.

The kids were ready for the pool and were soon fully immersed in the water. I dipped my toe in the shallow end and was quite taken aback by the freezing temperature. These kids like most other children didn't appear to feel the cold. I on the other hand felt that a dip in the icy cold water was at least two hours too early to contemplate. For me the sun needed to heat up the pool until midday at least.

This was a nice idea in theory, but one that wouldn't materialise, because within seconds I'd joined the two children in the deep end of the pool.

To say I was now wide awake was an understatement; every nerve in my body was awake. There were nerves in my body that I never thought I had that were wide awake.

It was far too early for this type of activity and certainly far too cold, but I was up to the task. We started to have a game of catch with a ball and very soon my body had adjusted to the freezing water. I was now starting to enjoy myself, and there was no doubt that the kids loved it too. So much so that they appeared to forget about their mothers plight.

However, I was very much thinking about their mother. I hoped she was on the mend and hoped that we would be in a fit state to spend a lot more time with me in the not too distant future.

The pool was starting to fill up with the other children in the hotel, although it was still much too early and still far too cold for the rest of the *normal* adults.

I noticed that the party from *Planet Knob-head* were beginning to surface and starting to make their usual din. They were taking a whole corner of the poolside loungers for their own. At least sixteen of their towels were being draped over their chosen sun loungers. Half of the towels were red, white and blue, obviously containing the Union Jack as part of their design. It was tasteful stuff. *Not!* It made you proud to be British. *Not!* No wonder we are the envy of the Western World!

The whole Union Jack theme was also visible in several of the swimming costumes worn by the group. Two of the men wore long shorts with the familiar design and one of the ladies wore a bikini with the same national pride evident for all to see.

It was hideous to behold and quite frankly I needed to be elsewhere. In a panic stricken moment I suggested to the kids that we should maybe have a walk to the beach instead of playing in the pool. Their faces told me in an instant that they much preferred to stay where they were.

There was no escaping at that particular time, I would have to grit my teeth and grin and bare it.

Another hour passed. There weren't any mirrors around the pool so I couldn't check my reflection, but I'm guessing that throughout the hour my grin was one of gritted teeth. I must have looked pretty strange.

Around midday Teri arrived with some refreshments for the three of us.

'Feeling any better?' I enquired.

'A little better, thanks.' came the reply. Although the slightly pale colour in her face suggested otherwise.

We were pretty hungry after our exertions over the last few hours and the kids and I were grateful for the pit stop.

'Do you fancy a coffee from the pool bar?' Teri asked.

'Yeah thanks, but I'll get them, you relax. What do you want?'

'I'll have an ordinary coffee thanks.' she said.

I walked over to the pool bar and placed my order for two coffees. I started chatting to the lady serving me.

'Lovely children you've got there.' she said.

'Oh they're not mine; in fact I've only known them for a few days.'

She looked surprised and continued to pour the coffee and a small jug of milk.

She continued to say, 'by the way you were all playing together I just assumed they were yours. You look so natural with them.'

'Oh I've had kids of my own' I said. 'I just love kids; I guess I'm still one myself.' She smiled warmly.

At that moment my mind was transported back to happier times, playing with my own kids on numerous holidays, mainly in the UK. We'd spent a lot of time at Center Parcs when the kids were younger, which we loved. Marie was a great mother and we all got on so well. The four of us against the world and all that. The kids had moved on now and of course Marie and I started to have problems. The thought of it all was still painful for me. Over the last year or so I had become pretty hardened to it all and had learned to avoid the trap of thinking too much. It usually ended in tears. Mine.

The voices in my head were now getting more vocal: *'It's over. Why do you punish yourself? She's never coming back.'*

I snapped out of the trip down memory lane when a loud blast of Yorkshire shot across the poolside. 'What are you playing at? The coffee'll be cold.'

'Yeah sorry, I was miles away.' I grabbed the drinks off the counter and left the appropriate change in the saucer whilst nodding to the lady who'd served me.

Missing the Plot

We drank our coffee and talked for a while as the kids finished off their sandwiches and crisps. 'So what are you planning for us today Ed?'

I quickly realised that I hadn't given today any thought whatsoever and to be fair I was in need of a rest. I was feeling a bit under the weather myself after last nights over indulgence. I looked at Teri and the kids and thought what the hell.

'Well, what do you fancy doing?' I asked.

'We could go to the beach.' Teri suggested.

The kids overheard this and started to get excited. 'Yes let's go to the beach mummy.' said Mattie with a huge grin.

'The beach, the beach.' Lucy echoed.

'Ed's coming too mummy isn't he?' Mattie said.

Teri turned to me and smiled. 'You've got an admirer'. At that moment Lucy jumped up onto my lap and put her arm around my neck. Teri smiled again and simply said, 'sorry, *two* admirers.'

'The beach it is then.' I said to the absolute and obvious joy of the two children.

Chapter Thirteen

After all the gathering of bits and bobs, and then the gathering of certain bobs that she'd forgotten in the first place and a few bits that she eventually decided she'd also need, we were ready for the beach.

I was packed to the hilt like a donkey, Teri had a bag in each hand and the kids were also carrying various towels and playthings.

'How long are we going for again?' I joked.

'You're out of practice Ed; you really do need to take all of this stuff.' Teri replied.

I remembered back to similar times and similar scenarios with Marie and my own kids and realised she was right.

'No I remember Teri, it wasn't that long ago.' I said.

She just smiled.

We arrived at Fig Tree Bay at 1.15 and the beach was full of holidaymakers. I pointed with my head, it's the only thing I could point with, to a spot near some empty sun loungers. We trundled across the sand and made our way to the place that would become our base for the next three or four hours.

Teri made sure the kids were protected by sun cream, as the sun was really hot at this time of day. Happy that they were well protected Teri let them race off towards the sea. The water at Fig Tree Bay was quite shallow and an ideal spot for the kids to play.

'Don't go too far Mattie and keep an eye on Lucy.' Teri called.

'Okay mummy.' he replied.

Teri and I laid out some towels.

'Will you do my back please?' She handed me the sun cream and I duly obliged. As soon as I'd finished applying the lotion on her back she turned to me and took the cream to return the favour saying: 'Right, I'll do yours.'

She rubbed the cream deeply into my back. I was enjoying the sensation and decided to have a little fun. 'Can you do the back of my legs while your there?'

'Yeah sure.' she said.

'Can you do the fronts as well?' I added cheekily.

'Ed, you can do your own front I'm sure.' she said. I couldn't see the look on her face but I guessed it included a smile. It usually did.

All of a sudden there was a scream that came from the edge of the water. It was Lucy. In an instant Teri was on her feet and speeding towards her daughter. I followed quickly behind. We arrived seconds later to see Lucy pointing out towards a rock. The rock was approximately thirty feet away and stood proudly about ten feet out of the water. On top of the rock was Mattie. He was obviously upset and in distress. Without hesitation I started to walk and then wade out towards him. The water was deeper than I'd anticipated and I arrived at the rock with the water level up to my chest.

'Are you okay Mattie? Are you hurt?' I asked with some urgency.

He just said, 'I'm stuck. I can't get down.'

'Don't worry mate, I'll get you down.' I looked up at Mattie on top of the rock in wonder. 'How did you get up there?' The rock was pretty high and didn't appear to have any hand or foot holds.

'I don't know, I just scrambled up. I was nearly drowning.'

'Mattie I don't know if I can get up there, can you jump? I'll catch you mate.'

'It's too high.' he said.

'I'll catch you.' I replied. 'I promise.'

'Promise?' he urged.

'After three' I said, 'one….two….'

Before I could get to three Mattie was heading right for me. I remembered our race on the giant slide and was about to smile when his left leg hit me right on the side of the head. Nonetheless I still managed to actually catch him, although it could also have been described as breaking his fall with the use of my head!

Under the force of the impact we both fell under the water for a moment. On surfacing I wiped the sea water from my eyes and held Mattie in my arms.

'You alright?'

'Yeah thanks.' he said, 'do you want to play ball?'

'Well maybe, but we'll just pop and see your mum for a bit; I think she needs a hug.'

I carried Mattie for a while then he started to walk himself and was soon in his mother's arms.

'What were you doing? I said not to go too far out.' she said anxiously.

'I was only playing.' the boy replied with a tear in his eye.

'Well be more careful please!' she said firmly. Teri turned to me and said thank you. She gently put her hand on the side of my head and said, 'you've got a bit of a bruise coming. How did that happen?'

'He didn't wait until three.' I said. 'I wasn't quite ready to catch him.'

'You poor thing.' she said. With that she leaned forward and kissed me on the cheek. 'Thanks again.'

After the incident things quickly settled down and I took Mattie up on his offer of play, we grabbed the ball and proceeded to have a game of catch.

I don't know what it is with boys and balls (if you know what I mean!) but there's always fun to be had.

Mattie was quite good at catching but his throwing technique was still somewhat lacking. Having said that it was still much better than all the girls I've ever known. What is it with girls and throwing? It's a real mystery! The female gender can do just about anything, apart from throw! Tessa Sanderson and Fatima Whitbread apart!

Lucy and Teri were making sandcastles near the edge of the water. Mattie threw the ball up in the air and I ran backwards to try to catch it. I hadn't realised I was so close to where the girls were playing and just as I was about to catch the ball I felt something give way under my feet. In typical fashion and doing my finest Mr Magoo impersonation I'd backed straight into their sandcastle, completely ruining their effort. Of course I felt instantly guilt-ridden and immediately apologised to the girls. But not only had I demolished their sandcastle I felt as though I'd pulled a muscle in the small of my back.

'I *can't* believe you….You're so accident prone.' Teri couldn't contain her laughter and I too saw the funny side of it.

Although, what with the bang on the side of my head from the incident earlier and the pain I was now feeling in my back, I didn't really feel like laughing.

'I think I'm falling for you Teri.' I said jokingly.

She just looked at me with a big beaming smile. The smile broke into a laugh again and this time all four of us joined in.

The rest of the day went by without too much incident. Mattie and I played some football, I took both kids for a swim and we all rebuilt the sandcastle, this time on a much grander scale. I like to think my years in the building trade helped and Mattie in particular was impressed with my design. It was quite simply a really enjoyable hour or so and it took me back to numerous seaside holidays I'd been on with Marie and the kids.

Sometime later it was getting late and we decided to head back to the hotel.

'Wow, my jaws ache.' Teri said, 'I haven't laughed so much in ages.'

'Yeah, usually at me!' I said. 'But I don't mind, I'm really enjoying myself.'

I hadn't had so much fun in ages myself and I had to admit to myself that I'd really taken a shine to this family. The kids were great and their mother was right up my street. She was pretty, smart and a really nice person. I'd made a bit of a joke of it at the time, but I was falling for her. I was seriously falling for her.

'I think the kids and I are staying in for tea tonight, I've got loads of food in and I was going to make a jacket potato and salad. There's plenty…You're welcome to join us.'

I thought for a moment and smiled at her. 'That would be lovely. What time shall I come round?'

'Oh make it an hour.' she said.

'Great, I'll see you then.' I replied.

I was totally knackered and a little bruised. My back was still aching and there was a small bump on the side of my head. It was nothing too serious, but I did look as though I'd been in the wars rather than playing on the beach with a couple of kids.

I got back to the room, had a shave and shower and changed into something smart but casual. I decided that I'd pop to the supermarket and grab a bottle of wine and something for dessert. In the end I settled on a small strawberry ice-cream sundae, I figured you couldn't go wrong with that.

After an hour or so I knocked on their door with the bottle of Shiraz and the dessert in hand. Mattie opened the door and I could see that the room was in total chaos. Apparently Teri had crashed out in the bedroom and had snoozed off. The kids were happily playing and all the stuff from the beach was spread around the room.

Teri had obviously just woken and was frantically trying to put things away and prepare the potatoes for the meal.

'Need a hand?' I asked.

'Do you mind, I need shower. The salads in the fridge, I've got the jacket spuds in the microwave and I was just about to grate some cheese. Thanks Ed.' And with that she disappeared to the bathroom to have a shower. I just looked at Mattie who simply shrugged his shoulders.

I opened the bottle of wine to breathe and started on the salad. When the potatoes were nearly done I stuck them in the oven to crisp them up. All of this was a doddle for me; I'd been on my own for over a year and was more than capable of making a simple meal.

Thirty minutes later the potatoes were ready and as it happened it was at that moment that Teri finally joined us.

She looked refreshed and very pretty. She'd caught the sun and was glowing in more ways that one. I poured us a glass of wine and passed a glass to Teri.

'Thanks, you're a star.' she said.

'Ed's brought some ice-cream for afters mum.' Mattie said with obvious delight. I smiled at him.

'You never cease to amaze me.' Teri said 'I might just have to take you home with us.'

'Who wants cheese on their potato?' I said. They all immediately made it clear that it was a "yes" all round.

The meal was pleasant enough, but the ice cream sundae stole the show. We all wolfed it down. Afterwards we watched a bit of TV and then Teri said, 'It's time for you two to get ready for bed.'

The kids of course objected for all they were worth. But their mother was resolute and their protests fell on deaf ears. Reluctantly they brushed their teeth, donned their pyjamas and retired to the bedroom.

After settling them down for ten minutes or so Teri returned to join me on the settee. 'You know I really can't thank you enough Ed.'

'Teri it's my pleasure. You and the kids have made my holiday.'

'How's the book coming along?' Teri asked.

The book! I'd come to Cyprus to write a book. I'd forgotten all about the book.

'Oh it's still in the planning stage.' I said. 'I might need to pick your brains about a couple of things.'

'You'll send me a copy when its done won't you?'

'Of course I will, when it's done.'

I realised that the whole book idea was a bit *"pie in the sky"*. I hadn't really done any work on it. I'd thought about it, and I'd basically settled on a possible plot, but I'd not actually started it yet.

The voices started to tease me: *'You're more interested in this lady aren't you? You'll never finish the book. You'll probably never even start it. It's yet another thing you couldn't do.'*

I shook away the thoughts and poured us both another glass.

'Go easy Ed, I'm still a bit tender from last night.'

'Take your time Teri, there's no rush. Hey do you fancy watching the X Files?' It was just about to start on TV.

'Yeah I love the X Files. It's one of my all-time favourites.' she said.

'Me too.'

Somewhere deep within me I heard: *'It's another sign!'*

I'd seen the episode before and I think Teri had too. Still, it was a good one and we both enjoyed it again. It was getting late and was starting to get much cooler. I mentioned this to Teri and she agreed and quickly suggested a solution: 'Why don't you snuggle up to me?'

I didn't know if it was the wine talking or not, but I didn't need to be asked twice. I moved closer to her and put my arm around her shoulder.

'Teri do you mind me saying something?'

'No, go ahead.' she replied.

I was feeling quite confident but at the same time I was conscious that I didn't want to come on too strong. I didn't want to spoil anything.

'I think you're great and I really want to kiss you right now.'

There, I'd said it. My heart was racing and I felt a little bit nervous about her response. But I was also feeling quite excited to be here with this lovely lady.

'If you're going to kiss me I suggest you get on with it!' she ordered.

'Modern women eh!' I said and I gently held her head in both hands and kissed her. Her mouth was open and she tasted sweet. Our tongues brushed and I felt a warm feeling inside. The kiss lasted for ages and I only paused to come up for air. I looked her deeply in the eyes and could see my reflection looking back at me.

'I've wanted to do that for ages.' I said softly.

'And I've wanted you to.' she replied, 'for days.'

'Wow, what's happening Teri?'

'Ed, some things are meant to be, just enjoy it.' With that she moved towards me and kissed me long and hard. It was wonderful and filled with passion and at the same time a tenderness that took my breath away.

However, this was the first kiss I'd had in a long time. The first time I'd kissed another woman other than my wife in over twenty years. It felt exciting but at the same time I was feeling guilty.

'Why are feeling guilty you fool. She left **you** *remember. Snap out of it and live your life.'*

The voices were resolute and determined that I should continue kissing this wonderful creature before me. But they don't always get their own way and this was one of the times they wouldn't.

'Teri, I'm sorry but I'm gonna call it a night. You don't mind do you?'

'But I thought that…' She stopped in mid sentence.

'I'm sorry, I just can't. It's too soon for me.'

She simply said okay and pecked me on the cheek..

'There's no rush.' she whispered, 'and anyway I'm tired myself.'

'Maybe we can do something tomorrow?' I asked. 'With the kids.' I quickly added.

'Let's see how we feel in the morning eh?'

I said that was a good idea and thanked her for her company and added that she was a very nice kisser. She smiled and put her finger on my lips and said 'I could tell you were a bit nervous, but you've got potential in the kissing stakes, bags of potential!'

I thanked her and said I was a bit nervous because I was half expecting a head butt. We both laughed and said our good nights.

As I walked over to my room I was deep in thought. Who was I kidding? The reason I couldn't carry on kissing her was when I looked deep into her eyes it wasn't Teri looking back at me, it was Marie.

Chapter Fourteen

I didn't sleep too well that night. My head was full of many thoughts. I was thinking about Teri and how much I liked her and I was thinking of the lady that had been my partner throughout more than half of my life.

I was sure that I'd moved on in my heart and in my head. I was sure that our time was over. But for some reason that neither of us could explain we were still really good friends and we were still very much married. Yes, we'd been separated for a while, but nothing more than that.

Throughout our early separation we'd sent each other many texts that had tried to show our true feelings. I didn't need to strain my memories for their content I'd saved every one. They talked about "true love" winning in the end. In the early days I'd believed wholeheartedly in the sentiments, but after a while the strength of feeling began to fade somewhat, although I'd still retained the messages on my phone. Why had I done that? Was it to punish myself? I didn't know the answer. I just knew that erasing them was possibly the final act and I hadn't been quite ready for that.

The Cyprus morning was bright, but I didn't feel too cheerful. My mind went back to the previous night and the way I felt when I was kissing Teri.

It was wonderful and I'd really enjoyed our closeness. However, at the same time I had felt so very guilty.

'You've got to move on, got to let go.'

I wasn't sure how to approach Teri this morning. Maybe I needed to give her some space; maybe I needed some space myself. In the end I decided that I would give the book some thought.

I plugged in the lap top and typed the title of the book. The title "Missing the Plot" seemed to sum up everything in my life at the moment. My marriage was on the rocks, my book was a non starter and the friendship with Teri was almost certainly at an end. She must have thought I was a total loser.

I typed what I thought would be the opening line: "I was going to Cyprus for one reason and one reason only, to write a book."

I liked the way it sounded and continued writing about how they say that everyone has a book in them and that I felt that this was pretty lame because so many people I know obviously haven't got the know-how to write a book.

I liked how the words sounded and continued writing for a few hours more.

Some time later there was a knock on my door. I carefully placed the lap top to one side and opened the door to reveal Teri and Lucy.

'Hi there, how are you?' I enquired.

'We thought you'd gone home.' Teri said playfully

'No no, I've just been working on the book.'

'Oh how's it going, are we disturbing you?'

'No.' I lied 'I was just finishing off. What are you guys up to?'

'The kids were thinking about going to the beach again. I'm not so sure. It's a bit daunting on my own.' I could sense she was hinting for me to join them and it has to be said she was none too subtle about it.

'I could tag along if you like.' I suggested with what must have seemed like a degree of reluctance in my voice.

Teri obviously sensed this and immediately her tone changed to one slightly more irritated. 'Well I wouldn't want you to do something you didn't want to do.'

In actual fact I was more than happy to join them and anyway I'd lost my train of thought regarding the book and was in need of a break.

'Teri I wouldn't suggest it if I didn't want to do it. I'd love to join you.'

Her mood lifted immediately and she smiled.

'Well, grab your stuff we're going in five minutes.' she announced.

'Five minutes?' I said, 'I'll meet you at the poolside then.'

Of course I figured I had at least fifteen minutes and calmly gathered my swimming trunks, towel and various necessities. However, being the sort of man I was I still didn't want to be late and arrived at the poolside in the allotted time.

Mattie was sat on one of the loungers with a pile of bits and bobs, but the two girls were nowhere to be seen.

'Mum said she won't be long, Lucy needs the toilet.' he told me.

'Okay mate, no worries.' I replied.

Ten minutes later they appeared. 'Toilet duty!' Teri confirmed.

'So I understand, ready to go?'

'Ready when you are.' she said.

'Bite your tongue, bite your tongue.'

Without any further delay we gathered all our things and headed once again for the beach at Fig Tree Bay. I gently rubbed the side of my head and promised myself to take it easier today.

Things had shifted slightly between Teri and I but it was obvious that neither of us had a problem with it. I smiled at Teri and I was pleased we were still getting on well and the way that Teri smiled back at me suggested she felt the same.

We arrived at Fig Tree Bay to the sound of the motor boat pulling the inflatable banana and with the look on the kids' faces it was on their list of things to do for the day.

'Mummy can we go on the banana boat? Can we please mummy?'

'We'll see, maybe if you behave yourselves.'

'Does that include me?' I enquired with my tongue pressed firmly into my cheek.

'Do you think you can behave yourself for long enough?' she retorted.

Touché, I thought. She's got me there. I smiled in a deliberately childish way and promised to be a good boy, just for her.

Mattie and I played for a little while and throughout this time the young lad was forever looking longingly out to sea, towards the banana boat activity.

A short time later Teri wandered over to us and said, 'come on then you two; let's put you out of your misery. It's banana boat time!'

Mattie was visibly excited and started whooping and cheering. I tried to keep my cool, but inside was quite excited myself and the truth be known a tad nervous too. I had noticed that the driver of the boat tipped over the inflatable banana, thus ejecting the riders at what looked to be the point furthest out to sea.

I had to admit that this particular part of the ride was something I was dreading. The thought of it transported me back to a traumatic childhood memory, one I'd shared with my Dad in the mid 70's.

We queued for ten minutes or so and then the time arrived. We were all given life jackets as a safety precaution and I needed the biggest one they had. It's not that I'm overweight you understand; I'm just not keen on anything that's tight fitting. It feels uncomfortable and also makes me look fatter than I actually am! We waded out to where the banana boat was waiting and all four of us scrambled on board along with six other passengers of various ages.

I was sat right at the back of the banana with Mattie directly in front of me and with Teri and then Lucy in the positions ahead of the boy.

The motor boat set off and whilst the speed we reached wasn't going to break any records it was still exhilarating especially for the little ones.

We reached the point at which I had noted that the tipping of the passengers occurred and I gripped the sides of the inflatable tightly with my thighs. I wasn't going to be easy to dislodge off this particular banana boat.

The driver was skilled in this tipping manoeuvre and as far as I could tell he always achieved his goal. My childhood memory was kicking in and my thighs were getting ever tighter, it was gripping in more ways than one!

Then the driver quickly spun the motor boat in the opposite direction, causing the long yellow inflatable to tip over. Every other one of the passengers was dislodged in a split second, except me. My incredibly strong thigh muscles saved the day; there would be no dunking for me, or so I thought. Unfortunately the weight of me on the back only served to flip the thing upside down, meaning I was now completely underwater. Picture the scene; there I was still gripping onto the inflatable banana with my ultra strong thighs whilst upside down in the deep blue sea. It was then that the music started playing in my head. It was the theme music from Jaws and my childhood trauma from the 1970's was back with me again.

It was only a second or two, but when you have a vivid imagination a few seconds can seem to last much longer. My grip loosened at the same time as the inflatable banana was being spun around into its upright position by several of the dislodged passengers, which resulted in me being flung several metres away. I was a little dazed and confused and everyone else was either scrambling back on board or being pulled up by friends or family. As for me I was hearing the music in my head even louder now. In my head the monster shark was almost upon me and I moved at Olympic speed back to the relative safety of the vessel. Then like a scene from *Flipper* I soared like a dolphin out of the sea and onto the back of the banana grabbing hold of Mattie and Teri. They both looked around at me in amazement.

'You're unbelievable.' Teri roared.

'I've been working on that move for a while now.' I said slightly out of breath.

'I think it still needs some work Ed.'

All I could do was squeeze out a strained smile, which instantly broke into smile of relief as the driver started to pull us back to dry land.

When we arrived back on terra firma and after I'd settled down a bit I began to tell Teri all about my childhood phobia. I blamed my Dad and said, 'fancy taking a nine year boy to see a film like that? I've been scared to death of water ever since. I'm even nervous in the public swimming baths for Gods sake!'

'You poor thing.' she said with what appeared like genuine sympathy. This was immediately put into question when she started to giggle and then scream with laughter.

After Teri had finally stopped laughing we were able to talk about my life long trauma, which to my horror had been played out in the Mediterranean Sea off the coast of Cyprus. It was just as if the shark was there with me again in 2008. Of course the monster fish had never really left my side since I'd seen the film in 1975. We were destined to be together in my head whenever I was immersed in water. You have a lot to answer for Mr Benchley and especially you Mr Spielberg.

Teri carefully listened to my story and was actually quite sympathetic. She understood that the fear was very real.

She suggested taking my mind off the ordeal with ice creams all round.

'Sounds good.' I said, 'I'll get them. I've had enough of man eating sharks for one day!'

'Okay, I'll have a choc-ice; the kids will have a lolly, make them strawberry if they've got them.'

'Your wish is my command, I'll be back shortly.'

I made my way to the nearest supermarket to get the treats. It was only a few minutes away and I'd be back in no time. However, whilst I was there I bumped into the two younger Cockney girls and started chatting. Several minutes went by and before I knew it I'd totally forgotten the reason I was at the supermarket. After quite a while longer I suddenly broke away from the conversation with a sudden realisation that I was there for a reason.

'Sorry ladies I've got to dash, I'm supposed to be on ice-cream duty. They'll think I've gone off to make my own.'

I grabbed the required mix of frozen desserts and handed over the five euros to the shopkeeper.

I made my way as quickly as possible back to the beach only to be greeted with a stare as icy as the contents of my plastic bag.

'Where have you been? You've been gone ages.'

'Oh I got talking to a couple of people from the hotel, sorry.' I replied.

'Who was that then?'

'You know, the two cockney girls.' I replied.

'I see.' Teri answered with a slight attitude in her voice, 'I guess you forgot about us?'

'Not at all.' I lied, 'just lost track of time. Anyway here you go.' I handed over the choc-ice and lollies and starting tucking into the cornetto I'd bought for myself.

'I would have had a cornetto if I'd have known.' Teri said.

'You can have mine if you like, I'm happy with a choc-ice.'

'No that's fine, but I would have had one if I'd have known.'

'Sorry Teri, but you said you wanted a choc-ice.'

She shrugged her shoulders and just said I know but I would have had a cornetto if I'd have known.

I felt that this conversation could have gone on for many more hours and was quite relieved when we all started to tuck into our various choices and quietly gobbled them up. The cornetto was delicious and it also served to numb the pain in my mouth, as a result of *biting my tongue!* All I could think about was just how difficult to please some people are.

Chapter Fifteen

The rest of the day went quite well, although I did begin to crave for some home comforts. I missed my Sky Plus, my comfortable double bed, but especially the space to breathe.

We arranged to have our evening meal together that night and it was suggested that we have it in the hotel bar. The food there was pretty good and the service was always very friendly.

We were due to meet at 7.30 and I intentionally arrived twenty minutes early in order to have a quiet drink. I ordered a pint of Keo and started a conversation with the lovely Yvonne. I could just about make out her Scottish accent and wherever I was unsure of exactly what she'd said I found that a warm smile and a nod of the head got me through.

The first pint went down pretty well and I ordered another, figuring that my Yorkshire threesome would be late anyway. I was still in deep conversation with Yvonne and half way down my second pint when I felt the tap on my shoulder, it was Teri.

'Are we interrupting you?' she enquired with a slightly playful hint of sarcasm.

'Blimey is it that time already?' I said, whilst looking at my watch. The time was precisely 7.30pm and I was quite shocked to see them having arrived on time. I tapped my watch with two fingers and held it to my ear, childishly checking it hadn't stopped. This behaviour seemed to annoy Teri somewhat and she made her way to one of the many free tables. I asked her what she wanted to drink and checked that lemonade for the kids was okay. She ordered a glass of Shiraz and confirmed that lemonade would be fine for Mattie and Lucy.

I took the drinks over to the table with a couple of menus and handed the wine to Teri and the lemonade to the kids.

'Are you okay?' I asked.

'Yes I'm fine Ed. I know you think I'm always late, but you want to try getting three people ready, not just one and you'll soon find out why I'm sometimes a little late.' I resisted the urge the say, *'SOMETIMES LATE!'* and instead said with an attempt at empathy, 'I understand. I'm only playing.'

'Yeah I know, but I think it's a little insensitive sometimes.'

'Teri, I'm sorry, I didn't mean to upset you.' I said in an attempt to put the matter behind us. I then suggested that tonight's "special" looked pretty good. It was a Cypriot Lamb Kebab dish with salad and jacket potato or chips. Teri turned up her nose and said she fancied something else and might go for the Moussaka.

'That sounds good to me. What about the kids?'

'Oh they'll have the same.' she said.

We ordered all of the meals and I suggested we order a bottle of the Shiraz to share. Teri nodded in agreement, our little misunderstanding already a thing of the past.

We ate our meals and the kids went off to play with another couple of English children in the play area leaving Teri and I to talk in peace. We were happily talking about nothing in particular when Teri asked a question that was to spurn a huge debate.

'Here's one for you.' she said, 'is it better to have loved and lost than never loved at all?'

'Ah, good question.' I replied. 'Now **that** is a difficult one.'

I went on to say that having "loved and lost" myself and experienced the real pain that comes with having done so, I reckoned that it was better never to have loved at all, because if you'd never loved at all you wouldn't feel the pain.

Teri took the opposite view: 'But surely it's better to have actually loved and lost than to never ever have the feeling of love in your life. If you went through life and never felt true love then surely that would leave a big hole?'

'Teri can I ask you a very personal question?'

'It depends how personal.'

'Well, the question is this, have you ever loved and lost?'

'No not really. Well, actually no, not at all.' she replied.

'Well in that case I hardly think you're in a position to comment on this. I have certainly loved and absolutely lost. Trust me Teri you're better off living a life of ignorance than a life of pain.'

She looked visibly hurt by my sentiments and strength of feeling on the matter and she began to make clear her own feelings with much more passion and vigour.

'Ed just because I haven't been in love doesn't mean that I can't have an opinion on this.'

'I know, I know.' I said defensively.

She went on, 'and just because you've been in love and it all went wrong doesn't mean you are the world's foremost expert on the subject.'

She was right of course and I wanted to say she was right, but a part of me also wanted to argue.

'Look all I'm saying Teri is that if you haven't lived through the pain it's hard to give an informed opinion. You're just looking in on someone else's pain and you can't possibly know how they feel.'

'Okay, okay you've made your point. You're right and I'm wrong.' she said with a slightly raised voice.

I didn't want to argue at all, but I felt strongly that you had to live through the pain of losing the love of your life to understand this.

'Teri it's not about me being right or you being wrong, but I do feel that you can only really understand the answer if you've really understood the question and to do that you've got to have lived through it.'

As I said it I knew it sounded pompous and righteous and instantly regretted how it came out. The result was that Teri said nothing in response and we just sat in silence for several minutes. I had completely pissed her off and she was letting me know how much with the look on her face.

After a few more minutes she simply said, 'the problem with you Ed is that you obviously still love your wife, so the truth is that you aren't capable of having this discussion because you're still in pain from the loss.'

'She's right', said the voices from within.

'Maybe you're right Teri.' I said, 'maybe you're right.'

She gave me a look that suggested she thought that she was right and we sat in further silence as we both metaphorically licked our wounds. Teri felt patronised and belittled by my stubbornness to accept her opinion on the subject and I felt as though someone had taken a pair of giant tweezers and started to pick at the scab that I thought was well on the way to healing. How wrong I'd been on that one.

I eventually swallowed my pride and broke the silence by asking Teri whether she wanted another drink. She thought for a brief moment and said, 'why not? I'll have a Bacardi and coke.'

I nodded my head in appreciation of her suggestion and headed to the bar to order the same for both of us.

By the time I'd returned to the table we'd both calmed down a bit and Teri said, 'it's only a difference of opinion. It's not worth falling out over.'

I agreed and suggested we call a truce. Teri smiled and she raised her glass and clinked my own as she said the word, 'truce.'

At that moment the kids returned asking for another drink, I duly obliged.

Mattie started yawning and I sensed that the evening was coming to an end.

'Is it bedtime?' I asked.

'Yeah I think so; the kids are shattered after a long day.'

'I'll walk you back to your room if that's okay?'

'Thanks, that would be nice.'

'Hey Teri I'm sorry to have been such a pillock, but I guess you're used to it in one way or another.'

She smiled and said that she wouldn't hold it against me. I just smiled in return and we headed back to their room. When we arrived I went in for a few moments to check that everything was fine. Teri asked me if I wanted to watch some TV. I said it was probably best that I get off and that I'd maybe see them tomorrow.

'Hey Teri you know I think you're great don't you?' I said, 'and I hope when we get back to the UK we can keep in touch and maybe even meet up.'

Her face seemed to light up at my suggestion and she said, 'that would be nice. Are you sure you won't stay for a while?'

Whilst I was very tempted to sit and watch some TV with this lady I was also feeling pretty well shattered myself. It had been a long day and quite draining for me. I reiterated that it was probably time to call it a night and once again thanked her for the kind invitation. I said my good-nights to the kids and bent forward to kiss her on the cheek. As my mouth reached the side of her face she turned towards me, intentionally this time, and my kiss that was intended for her cheek found itself planted on her lips instead. We both held it for a few seconds and then pulled away gently. Our eyes met and we both gave a smile of realisation.

'Listen, I've got a bottle of Chardonnay in my fridge if you want to share a glass, what do you say?'

Teri's smile broadened and she simply said, 'what a good idea. I'll sort out the kids while you go and get it.'

So much for an early night I was thinking as I wandered back to my room to gather the wine. But I was nearly the end of my Cyprus adventure and I was being driven on by several voices saying, *'you only live once'*.

I decided to freshen up slightly and proceeded to brush my teeth, change my shirt and to finish off I sprayed a little after shave in all the right places.

I grabbed the cooled bottle of wine and headed back to Teri's room. She had left the door very slightly ajar just in case she was in the middle of settling the kids. I walked in, grabbed a couple of wine glasses and poured us both a drink. I then switched on the TV and checked to see if there was anything worth watching on the few channels that occasionally had English speaking programmes.

We were in luck, because in twenty minutes time a film was due to start. I'd seen it before but it was an half decent film called *Enemy of the State* with Will Smith and Gene Hackman, the latter being one of my favourite American actors and of course Will Smith was always very watchable.

After ten minutes or so Teri joined me on the sofa and I informed her of the film that what was about to start.

'Oh I think I've seen it, but I can't remember what happens.'

I was instantly reminded of Marie. She was always saying things like that and there were countless occasions over the years when we watched many films that she'd swore blind she'd never seen until the final few frames when she suddenly remembered that we **had** seen them.

I used to say, 'trust me we've seen it!' and she'd reply, 'I'm certain I haven't seen it, you must have seen it with someone else.'

I was suddenly back in Teri's room in present day Cyprus and mentally giving myself a hard time for thinking about Marie again. Teri had obviously seen the angst on my face and asked if I was okay. I assured her I was and lied that I was thinking about an idea for the book.

'Oh the book, how's it going then?'

'Well I'd settled on a romantic comedy type of plot, but so far its more like a comedy romance, trouble is it's not very funny!'

'Oh dear Ed, I hope the comedy romance hasn't been inspired by me at all.'

My immediate reply was: 'Teri, you inspire *romance* in me, but certainly not comedy.' I hoped it came out the right way and the look she gave me suggested that my line was well received and I decided to carry on with the flirtation.

'I've really enjoyed meeting you Teri.' There was a slight pause, 'and the kids!' I quickly added.

'You've all made my holiday. I guess it's meant that I've not worked much on the book, but to be honest I'd much rather have spent my time with you.' Again as an afterthought I added, 'the **three** of you.'

'I've, well, we've enjoyed meeting you too Ed. It's been fun. You're a nice guy.'

'Ah, so I am a nice guy after all?' I teased.

'Yes I guess so, when you're not being a pillock anyway.'

'Ouch!' I said, 'sorry about that, but I'm pleased for you that you've actually met one.'

'What's that?'

'A nice guy Teri.' And I reached for the bottle and topped up our glasses.

We started watching the film and continued to drink the wine.

'It's getting a bit chilly don't you think?'

'Ed, don't beat around the bush. If you want to put your arm round me just do it.'

I wasn't used to women being so modern and so forward. When I was first courting it would have taken me the best part of an hour to successfully complete the "arm around the girls shoulder" technique. Nowadays it seemed that the girl grabbed your arm and stuck it over her own shoulder for you in double quick time. As Mr Dylan famously said: "Times they are a changing."

Still, looking on the bright side this new updated method did save an awful lot of time!

I shuffled closer to Teri and held her tightly while we were still watching the film. Then I turned to look at her and as she was still engrossed in the action on the screen I gently kissed her on the side of her head. She turned to me and smiled.

'Ed, the kids are still stirring a bit, you need to be patient.'

'Oh Teri, I was only giving you a peck, I'm actually enjoying the film.' Of course the truth was I was getting pretty bored with the film and I just wanted to hold her tighter and kiss her fully on the lips.

'Okay, but you're starting to get that "aroused man" look about you and you can't stop bloody fidgeting.'

'Aroused man look?' I repeated, 'what the heck's that?'

'I suggest you look in the mirror, you'll see what I mean.'

'Teri it takes more than an arm round a pretty girls shoulder to get me aroused. I think you're confusing aroused with interested.' The problem was of course when a man starts to talk to a woman about the fact that he might be getting aroused, it usually only served to arouse him. Teri had also uncovered another one of my many foibles; the more I started to get aroused the more I started to fidget!

Another foible was that the fidgeting led to a need to feed my face. I was starting to get quite peckish and was hoping that with two children around there would be loads of savoury titbits. The stark reality was, had we been in my room the only late night feast I could have offered would have been Kellogg's Fruit and Fibre!

Anyway my stomach was beginning to rumble and I cheekily enquired about the possibility of a late night snack. Teri took her eyes off the TV for a second and gestured towards the kitchen units. 'There's a few nibbles in the left hand cupboard if you want some, on the top shelf.'

'Sounds like a plan.' I replied and quickly grabbed a packet of the local salt and vinegar crisps for us to share.

I joined her back on the sofa; she looked at me and playfully said, 'now can you relax for the rest of the film?'

'I'll do my best. But I can't promise.' Without hesitation I immediately placed my arm around her shoulder again. I was getting used to this modern approach.

We just sat and watched the film and I actually enjoyed it in the end. But I also really enjoyed the closeness I felt to Teri, not just closeness due to proximity, but an emotional closeness that was growing between us. We'd only known each other for just under a week but we'd spent a lot of time together, along with the kids. I really was starting to feel something for this lady.

After the film had finished Teri popped to the toilet and when she returned she sat next to me and looked me straight in the eyes. Her eyes were a bluey green colour and were so wide and beautiful.

'Your eyes are beautiful.' I couldn't help but say it.

'Thank you, but you do realise that sounds like a line.' she said.

'Well it may sound like a line, but trust me it isn't and I really do mean what I say, you have stunning eyes.'

This time when she said thank you I could tell that she meant it with more sincerity and that she'd accepted that my compliment was genuine.

'We *will* try to catch up back in the UK won't we?' I said testing the water.

'I don't see why not.' she replied. 'I like you and the kids think you're cool.'

My chest started to poof out and I smiled one of those smug smiles that suggest you're very proud of yourself. 'They think I'm cool eh? That's pretty, dare I say, cool!'

She shook her head in a *there's no hope for him* sort of way and smiled back at me.

I asked if she minded me kissing her. She shook her head, smiled and then cheekily asked if I'd prefer a head butt.

'I'm pretty sure I'd prefer to kiss you Teri, but thanks for asking.'

We moved toward each other and slowly touched lips. Her skin was silky smooth and the scent of her perfume was divine. We kissed passionately and I felt sure that if I looked in the mirror at that moment then I'd see a man that looked somewhat aroused!

Just at that time when I thought that something was going to happen here, something happened. However, it wasn't the something that I had in mind, because at that moment the bedroom door swung open and Lucy burst into the lounge area with tears in her eyes. She was complaining of a tummy ache and was in some discomfort. Teri immediately broke away to tend to her daughter and within seconds Mattie also appeared in the doorway.

'Teri can I do anything?' I asked with some sympathy.

'Sorry Ed, there's not a lot you can do. Lucy just needs her mummy, don't you sugar plum?' she addressed the question to Lucy and the child simply nodded in reply.

It suddenly hit me that I was surplus to requirements here and I needed to leave them to it.

'Teri shall I leave you to it?' I suggested.

'It's probably for the best, sorry.' she answered. 'I'm really sorry.' she added.

'Okay, I understand. You know where I am if you need me.' And with that I wished her goodnight. Under the circumstances I didn't think a goodnight kiss was appropriate. It seemed that with one thing or another we were destined to stay at first base.

Back at my room I was once again riddled with guilt, even though nothing had happened. Deep down I'd wanted something to happen, but at the same time was mightily relieved it hadn't. But I was basically a single man, although I was still technically married, this was purely a technicality. I'd been separated from Marie for over a year. She'd left me for over a year ago. The voices started to ask questions: *Why are you feeling guilty? When are you going to get on with your life? Why does she still have this hold on you?*

I couldn't answer any of the questions. I never could. All I knew is that something was stopping me from moving on. Was I still grieving for my marriage? We'd been together for so long and we'd been happy for the vast majority of time. It was like losing your best friend, your lover, your partner and your soul mate all rolled into one.

All I could do at that moment was do what I'd done for so many nights in the last year, I cried myself to sleep.

Chapter Sixteen

I didn't sleep too well that night. I'd been thinking about Marie and why it had all gone so sour.

I looked in the mirror and never mind an aroused man what I saw was the reflection of a broken man, still that could have been the puffy eyes and lack of sleep. But there was no doubt I would need a good hour before the rest of the human race would accept me as part of their fold.

I poured myself some cereal and it was apparent that my holiday was coming to an end, I'd packed just enough for my time away and I reckoned there were two more portions after today.

I put the kettle on and made a coffee, discovering that the coffee supplies were also running low for the same reason.

I switched on the lap top and decided to have a go at typing something. There were lots to go at, I had actually fallen for a young lady and grown very fond of her children. But no matter how much I tried I couldn't get beyond thinking about the events of the week, putting them into words was a hopeless task.

Missing the Plot

As soon as I thought I had the germ of an idea my thought process was distracted by something else, it was usually Marie.

After thirty long minutes of fruitless writing I abandoned the idea. I decided to shave and shower and face the outside world, whether it was ready for me or not.

Twenty minutes later after my essential grooming I looked in the mirror and what I found looking back at me was bordering on acceptable.

I dressed in shorts and a short sleeved shirt and headed for the on site shop to get a little milk and water. Plus I'd decided to treat myself to a nice bread roll and a small pot of jam. Very few people were about and I was quite pleased for the relative peace and quiet.

I wondered what my friends were doing today, we hadn't made any plans and I really wasn't sure whether they would want to do the same thing again today as we did yesterday.

I didn't have long to wait before I saw one of the party because at that moment Mattie came into view. It appeared he too was on shopping duty to gather various supplies.

'Morning Mattie, how are you this morning and how's your sis?'

'Hi Ed, I'm okay, but Lucy's still poorly.'

'Oh dear I hope she recovers soon. Hey Mattie please tell your mum that if she needs anything just ask, okay?'

'Okay.' he said and then he disappeared into the shop.

I made my way back to the room and was now starting to salivate slightly at the thought of some jam on toast. Now if I looked in the mirror there was no doubt I'd definitely see an aroused man.

Thirty minutes later the telephone rang and I answered it cautiously, it was Teri.

'Hi Ed, just to let you know Lucy is still under the weather, but thanks for offering to look after Mattie.'

'Err okay.' I mumbled. I don't remember offering anything of the sort to the lad. He'd obviously mistaken my offer of help to Teri as an open help, or maybe it was a clever way of doing something more exciting than helping to look after his sick sister. I'd already thought that Mattie was a smart cookie; I definitely needed to add shrewdness to his list of attributes too.

'Well only if you're okay with it I mean.' I said with a little more conviction.

'Of course, that's fine; it's more than fine, thank you Ed. What are you planning on doing?' she enquired.

'Well it won't be the Banana boat you'll be pleased to know.' She just made a noise down the phone in agreement. 'I thought I'd speak to Mattie, but I was thinking about exploring the shoreline, rock pools and all that. Do you think he'd like to do some exploring?' I asked.

'He'd love that, he's a boy you know.'

I told her I'd worked that one out and went on to say that if he was anything like me he'd love to explore a bit of the island. 'I used to love doing that sort of thing with my Dad.' I quickly added, 'not that I'm trying to be his Dad!'

'I know you're not.' she said reassuringly. 'Trust me he'll love it.'

I asked Teri if she could have him ready in twenty minutes and she said no problem. *'We'll see,'* I thought to myself.

Earlier in the week I'd noticed quite a lot of rock formations and interesting little coves a little further down the coast from the Fig Tree Bay area and that was where I'd intended to start our little adventure. In fact I was starting to get a little excited myself at the prospect. What big kids like more than anything is to show off their skills and knowledge to little kids.

I remembered back to my Dad pointing out various types of fish and how to pick up a crab without being nipped, stuff like that. I was going to enjoy this little nostalgic adventure just as much as the boy.

I made my way over to their hotel room, skipping as I walked, whistling the theme from the Great Escape. Don't ask me why, it just came into my head and out through my pursed lips. I'm guessing I must have looked decidedly dodgy. It was probably a good thing Teri didn't witness this sight otherwise there was a good chance that she wouldn't let this strange man baby-sit her nine year old son.

I knocked on their door and before it had opened shouted in a playful voice, 'can Mattie come out to play?' The door opened and Teri stood there smiling. 'You're just a big kid aren't you?' she said warmly.

'Well it doesn't take a genius to work that one out. Is he ready to go?' At that moment Mattie appeared dressed ideally for what we were about to do. 'Are you ready mate?'

He nodded in confirmation. 'Let's do it then soldier.' I said in my best Sergeant Major voice.

We made our way down to the beach at Fig Tree Bay. My idea was to head down the coast a little towards the rock formations. The sun was beating down and thankfully we were both very protected with a generous amount of sun-cream. In fact we looked like a pair of anaemic ghosts; we were so smothered in the white lotion!

Fig Tree Bay was packed but I was hoping that it would be much quieter further down the coast line.

We arrived at a large mass of rocks just sitting in the sea some twenty minutes later. I asked Mattie if he was happy to climb to the top of it and he nodded and smiled a wide toothy smile.

I climbed up the first part and helped the boy up. He was adamant he could do it by his own steam and I admired his determination. It was an easy climb for me but because of his size and strength it was not that easy for the boy. However, he coped well and we reached the top and sat looking out to sea.

I pointed towards a shoal of fish that were about twenty feet away to the right of us. Several of the fish looked to be quite big. Then all of a sudden one of the bigger fish leapt out of the water in the middle of the shoal.

'Wow did you see that Mattie? What a whopper.' But the boy couldn't find the words and was transfixed and could only stare open mouthed at the sight.

Then he said, 'that's the biggest fish I've ever seen.' I looked down at him and said, 'your mum won't believe you. But I reckon it was two feet long.'

He smiled up at me with wide eyes and said, 'at least three feet!'

We watched the shoal move on, but there were no more fish acrobatics. Then we slowly climbed down from the rock and started to poke around in the many rock pools that were there.

Mattie was excited to see several crabs, a sea anemone and some smaller fishes. We removed our shoes and socks and paddled in the shallows for a while. It was all very pleasant.

We chatted about football and I was pleased that we supported the same football team. He was a Manchester United fan mainly because he adored Ronaldo. I could go back a lot further; I started to support them when Bryan Robson joined in the eighties.

I'm sure there was a generation that started to support them in the nineties when Cantana joined and indeed through the sixties with Charlton, Law and of course George Best.

You tended to be attracted by a certain player in a certain generation and we had that in common, although there was almost a thirty year gap between the particular players that had attracted each of us to the club.

The sun was getting hotter now and I suggested that we walk to the nearest café to get out of the sun for a while and have a drink.

'Can I have an ice cream instead?'

'Yeah no problem, lets head back to Fig Tree Bay, there's lots of places there.' Without a further word between us we turned and headed back.

I suggested a certain smart looking café and grabbed a table and asked Mattie what sort of ice-cream he wanted. He asked if he could see the menu and I nodded that was okay.

The waiter arrived with a couple of menus and after some deliberation Mattie chose a strawberry sundae and I ordered a pot of tea and a scone.

We feasted on our food and drink and talked some more about our favourite football team.

'We really need to get back Mattie, did you enjoy that?'

'What the ice-cream?' he replied.

'No, not just the ice-cream, the whole lot?'

'Yes, yes I did. Thanks Ed.' He sounded very grateful and I said he was very welcome and that I'd enjoyed it as much as him.

I paid the bill and we made our way back to the hotel. I said I hoped that his sister was feeling better. We arrived back fifteen minutes later and we went straight to Teri's room only to find it empty. I figured that Lucy must be feeling a bit better and they were probably around the pool. However, when we checked the poolside they were no-where to be seen. I checked in my pockets to find a couple of one euro coins and seeing that the pool table was free I suggested we have a game of pool. Mattie smiled and said that would be great.

I tried my best not to win, but it was not easy because Mattie found it difficult to make a bridge with his hand and could hardly pot a ball. I did what my Dad used to do when I was young and helped Mattie by making a bridge with my own hand so he could play a few shots and he actually potted three balls himself using this method.

In the end I got a little bored and cleared up my remaining three red balls and deposited the black in the middle bag. Of course the first thing Mattie said was, 'can we play again?'

I was very tempted, but suggested that we ought to try to find his mum and sister. He reluctantly agreed.

We didn't have to go very far because they arrived back at the hotel pool having just got back from a walk into Protaras. Lucy was looking healthier and Teri was looking her usual beautiful self.

'Hi Marie, where have you two been?' As the question came out I realised what a big mistake I'd made. I immediately backtracked and apologised and probably made the whole thing worse. 'I'm sorry Teri, old habits die hard.'

Teri looked a little annoyed by my accidental faux pa, but she just raised her eyebrows and changed the subject by addressing her son.

'Hey Mattie did you have a good time?'

'Fantastic mum we saw crabs and a massive shoal of fish. One jumped out of the water and it was five feet long.'

Without hesitation I added, 'well at least four feet I reckon.' I looked at Mattie and winked as I smiled. He attempted a wink which turned into a blink, but his returning smile was full of mischief. I really liked this boy.

But I was seriously annoyed with myself for saying Marie's name instead of Teri's. I'm sure there are very few things that irritate a person more then being called by the name of someone's ex. At least it wasn't whilst we were making love, which with our track record was hardly likely to be tested.

Chapter Seventeen

Tonight was my penultimate night in Cyprus, certainly for this particular holiday at any rate. I had enjoyed my time in Protaras and I was certain that I would be returning to the island again one day. Hopefully one day soon.

I was still feeling quite embarrassed by my slip of the tongue the previous night and there was little doubt that Teri was decidedly cooler towards me as a result of it. I didn't blame her one bit; it must really piss you off when that sort of thing happens. Can you imagine at the height of passion your partner screams out someone else's name? What a nightmare. Our example wasn't anywhere near as melodramatic as that, but nonetheless was equally ill timed and damaging to our budding friendship. It's hardly the type of thing that cements a relationship, unless the cement is cast around the bound legs of a relationship that is sinking in the Mediterranean Sea!

Anyway I knew that I had a lot of ground to make up, I knew I had to do something special to put this behind us if as I'd hoped we were to carry on seeing each other back home.

I decided on a three pronged approach, first of all I popped into Protaras and bought a nice bottle of Champagne and then I added the most expensive box of Belgian Chocolates in the shop. Surely both of those would go some way to getting me back in Teri's good books. Finally I popped into one of the classiest Italian Restaurants in town and booked a table for four for eight o'clock that evening.

I made my way back to the hotel and took the goodies back to my room and placed them in the fridge until later, when hopefully I would get the opportunity to give them to Teri.

I then changed into my swimming shorts and headed for the pool area. I found the Yorkshire trio around the poolside taking in the afternoon rays.

'How goes it...' before I could finish the sentence Teri felt the need to finish it for me with: 'It's **Teri**, by the way!'

I couldn't work out whether she was angry with me or just playing. I decided to ignore it, first rule of negotiation.

'Listen, I've taken the liberty of booking an Italian Restaurant tonight, my treat.'

No response.

'I remembered you saying you liked Italian and the kids seem to like pizza so I thought...' Again before I could finish she interrupted me again.

'Ed, I'm not sure what we're doing later, I'll let you know.'

I suddenly realized that the hole I was in as a result of last nights blunder was bigger than I'd originally thought. I almost started to defend myself, but decided to back down for now. 'Okay, well maybe let me know later then eh?'

She seemed to ignore me for a moment and then she eventually replied by simply nodding and smiling. But I had to admit it looked to be a slightly strained smile. It seemed I'd once again contrived to cock things up. As a result there was still quite a bit of making up to do and that seemed to sum up the story of my life.

It didn't take a fool to sense that Teri wanted some space for a while so I made my excuses and said I was popping into town for a few bits and I'd catch them later. I added, 'just let me know about tonight later, there's no hurry.' Teri agreed that she would.

I went into Protaras and spent half an hour at an Internet Café at the back of one of the many bars to check my emails and stuff. There were plenty of messages to check but actually nothing too important, mostly crap. Whilst I was there I noticed that there was a Karaoke from 7pm that night and that the first few punters to sing would get a drink on the house. I'd always fancied myself as a bit of a singer and once sang in a band in my teens and early twenties. The whole idea sounded very tempting and I decided that I'd play it by ear, although deep inside I was quite excited at the thought.

I made my way back to the hotel sometime later and the pool area was almost empty as the sun was starting to fall behind the buildings. I immediately noticed that Teri and the kids weren't there.

Back in my room I started to get ready and at about 6.30 picked up the phone to call Teri's room.

The phone rang five times and was picked up by Mattie.

'Hi Mattie, its Ed. Is your mum there?'

'Yeah I'll just get her.'

There was a brief silence as he went to get his mum and then she spoke.

'Hello Ed. Sorry we've got our own plans for tonight.' she said.

'Okay.' I said with a degree of hurt in my voice. 'Listen if you change your mind the Restaurant's called Emilios at the bottom of the main shopping street near Fig Tree Bay. The table's booked for eight.'

She made it clear that it was unlikely that they would change their minds. I immediately thought, *"**Your** mind Teri, your mind"*.

'Well have a good night then.' I said through gritted teeth, though I'm sure she couldn't hear the grit. At least I hoped she couldn't anyway.

I decided I would still go to the Italian Restaurant and maybe go a little earlier and earn a free drink at that nearby Karaoke Bar.

I had sung a lot in my time and was actually quite good, though I say so myself. However, I normally needed a few pints of Dutch courage to loosen my vocal chords. This was going to be different, this time I was looking to earn a pint after I'd sung rather than sink a pint or two before. Still, I was encouraged by the fact that not a soul in the sparse crowd knew me from Adam. I could be absolutely terrible and I'd still get a free pint and the good news was I'd never see a single person in this bar ever again.

I confidently made my way to the Karaoke host and asked if I could be one of the first. He nodded and enquired as to whether I'd chosen a song. I went with a popular song I knew quite well, "Daydream Believer" by The Monkies. If nothing else I could get the crowd singing along to the chorus.

'No problem mate, five minutes and you're on.' the slightly overweight but seriously jolly host announced.

'Oh shit.' I said to myself. All of a sudden it felt far too early and I felt far too sober to go ahead. I looked around at the faces in the crowd and found the courage to press on. The minutes ticked by and he handed me the microphone and said, 'it's a fairly quick intro so be ready.' I nodded that I understood his advice and waited for the music to start.

Then the title appeared on the screen and my body felt numb. It read "I'm a Believer" by the same group. The same group yes, but a totally different song, and one I was a bit unsure about. My confidence was fading fast and I turned in panic to the DJ. 'Excuse me mate, that's not my song.'

He nodded emphatically. 'Yes it is, that's what you asked for.'

'Daydream Believer!' I said, 'Daydream Believer!' With that the music started and I missed the first line. The crowd had obviously cottoned on to this bad start, but they were a supportive lot and I felt they were willing me to come good. I suddenly picked up the rest of the first verse, then the bridge and by the time the chorus kicked in we were all singing in unison.

At the end of the song I turned to the DJ and he said, 'good job mate, bit of a slow start, but you pulled it round.'

I didn't bother saying that it was him who had cocked it up by playing the wrong song. I just smiled.

'What are you having?' he said.

'I'll have a pint of Keo, thanks.' My throat was pretty dry and I was looking forward to that first long gulp. The lager arrived and went down without touching the sides.

I didn't do it very often but when I did, I always enjoyed a bit of Karaoke. It took me back to a time in my life when I didn't seem to have a care in the world. Our band played lots of gigs at all sorts of venues across the country and lots of girls in the audience fancied me. They were happy days.

The time was getting on and though I was tempted to stay and sing another song I decided I ought to move on to Emilio's and grab some food. It wasn't the night that I'd planned by a long chalk. I let out a long deep sigh and resigned myself to having a quiet meal for one.

I arrived at Emilio's and explained to the waiter that unfortunately only one of the Crawshaw party was here because the other members of the party were unwell. The waiter looked puzzled and said, 'but Sir your party are already seated, they are waiting for you.'

Now it was my turn to look puzzled and I assured him I was on my own.

He shook his head and pointed to a table at the far side of the restaurant. At the table there was one empty chair and one lady sat with two children. Of course it was Teri and the kids. I suddenly realised that Teri must have changed her mind.

I made my way over to the table and said hello.

'What time do you call this then?' she asked with a smile.

'I call it late.' I cheekily replied, 'but fashionably late, it's good to see you.'

She apologised for making such a big deal of my slip of the tongue and I said I understood how she must have felt and I didn't blame her for being miffed.

'Listen the main thing is you're here now, so let's have a good night eh?' I said with feeling. She agreed and we both smiled warmly at each other.

'Pizza, kids?' I asked excitedly and both of the kids nodded with great enthusiasm. 'What do you fancy Teri?' She looked at the menu for a few seconds and said, 'I fancy a spag bog.' I nodded in agreement. 'And do you fancy sharing a bottle of Shiraz?' she added.

'Good choice on both counts.' And I gestured for the waiter to come and take our order.

We laughed and joked and put yesterdays little problem right behind us. It was a lovely evening and the food was excellent. It was getting close to 10 o'clock and both kids started to get slightly bored and a little tired. I looked at Teri and with a knowing smile suggested that I get the bill. She agreed.

I decided I was going to treat them to dinner. My holiday was almost over and after cashing in my remaining travellers cheques I had plenty of euros to spend. Teri thanked me and said she would buy lunch or dinner tomorrow on my last day. I said I'd hold her to that.

'I'll take you guys back to the hotel.'

'That would be nice thanks.'

'My pleasure.' I said. I didn't want to mention the possibility of sharing more wine back at Teri's room and so said nothing. Teri stayed quiet on the subject too and we just talked about life back home in the UK on the way back to the Andreotis.

I walked them to their room and made sure everything was okay before leaving. Teri looked at me with anticipation in her eyes, as though she was willing me to take the initiative and invite myself to stay for a while. At least that's how it appeared to me, but I could have been wrong. However, I'd decided I wasn't prepared to make a mistake and be wrong on this one. I figured it was better to just go. My mind was made up and I decided to call it a night and kissed her on the cheek. As I did so I could almost taste the perfume on her neck and it made me feel quite heady. She had previously told me the name of the perfume was *Alien* and I have to say it was *out of this world* on her!

Back at my room I contemplated getting out the lap top and trying to do some work on the book. The thought soon passed and I opted to grab a beer out of the fridge and check out what was on the TV. On opening the fridge I immediately noticed the Champagne and chocolates and cursed to myself out loud. I took them both out of the fridge and thought about what to do next. There was only one thing for it, a little pacing was required. It was a bit like my favourite scene from *Love Actually*, when the guy who's in love with his best friends' new wife can't decide whether to tell her how he feels or not. He walks one way, then the other, then back again and then finally he says: 'Enough!' I love that scene.

In the same way I was going to Teri's room with the Champagne and chocolates, then I wasn't, then

I was again. In this case the scene would end in a different way when in my head a voice was heard to say: *'What have you got to lose? She's bound to be really impressed. Go for it!'*

That was it, my mind was made up. After a few minor adjustments and a little freshening up I was on my way with chocolates in one hand and a nice bottle of plonk in the other.

I knocked on the door and after a few moments a voice asked, 'hello, who's that?'

'Hi Teri, its Ed, listen I've got something for you that I meant to give you earlier.'

The door opened and Teri stood there in a pink and white pyjama set. She asked if I wanted to come in.

'Well, I've bought you a couple of things.' With that I handed over the Champagne and chocolates. 'It was part of my *sorry* for yesterday.' I added.

Teri took both the gifts and thanked me. She explained that the kids were just about settled and she was just about to watch a bit of TV and have a glass of wine.

'Hey, sorry to disturb you.' I said, 'I'll leave you to it. I just wanted to give you these.'

She thanked me again. I was feeling just a little stupid at that moment and was hoping that I didn't look as stupid as I felt.

'Hey, why don't you come and share a glass with me?'

All of a sudden I didn't feel so stupid and I'm sure my face must have lit up at the invitation.

'I'd love to.' I said with genuine gusto.

I made my way inside and complimented Teri on her outfit. She thanked me for the compliment and suggested I open the bottle and pour us a drink.

Teri then asked if I'd like a chocolate to go with the Champagne and I answered, 'well, maybe just the one.'

She shook her head and tutted. 'I can see you are one of those men that say *just the one*, but end up eating half the box!'

'Well if you insist.' I joked.

She opened the chocolates and we helped ourselves to a couple each. I was partial to a little chocolate with my wine and Teri seemed to enjoy it too.

'Thank you Ed. This was a nice thought.'

I said she was welcome and that it was the least I could do after last night.

'Ed, forget last night. It was one of those things.'

I changed the subject by saying, 'so what's on TV then?'

Teri muttered something about not knowing what was on, but not really caring anyway.

'Anyway, as you know I'm off home tomorrow evening, I just wanted to say how lovely it was to meet you and the kids.'

'Ed, I have to say that I've loved meeting you too. You're a lovely guy and you've made my holiday.'

I just smiled and said something really corny and thoroughly cringe worthy like she'd made my whole year!

We drank our first glass and I topped us up. We started to talk about life back home. I explained about my business interests and Teri talked about her study. I expressed my desire to catch up when we got back to the UK and Teri seemed to agree with the whole idea of it.

'I mean we're only just over half an hour from each other. It's nothing. In the big wide world, it's nothing.'

She nodded in agreement.

After another half glass we had demolished the bubbles and were both feeling pretty tipsy. I once again said how lovely she looked in her pink and white pyjama outfit and she smiled as she thanked me.

At that moment I was thinking about what she would look like "out" of her pink and white nightwear when something happened that would change the whole pattern of the evening. All of a sudden there was an incredibly loud sound of a bell ringing in the air.

'What the heck's that?' I screamed. It was loud enough to wake the whole hotel, and within a few minutes that's exactly what it did. Somewhere at the other end of the hotel complex one of the guests in a drunken stupor had accidentally set off the fire alarm whilst seriously burning their supper. The result was utter pandemonium and within several panic filled moments the whole hotel was gathered by the poolside in various states of undress.

Teri and I had gathered the kids within seconds and vacated the room. The minutes that followed were a huge source of amusement to us. The best laugh by far was the appearance of the *Knob-heads* with most of their party dressed in Union Jack nighties and pyjamas. I have to say even though I was still quite tipsy I almost wet myself, especially with the sight of the enormous beer bellies hanging in the cool night air. I remember saying to Teri that those ladies sure look sexy. She laughed a little too loudly, but nothing new there then.

A few moments later the hotel staff appeared assuring everyone that the hotel was not going to burn down and that everything was fine. I caught the eye of my cockney friends who asked how I was. I said okay and hoped they were too.

Shortly afterwards it was obvious that all was well and there was a suggestion from one of the cockney girls to have a night cap at the bar. I turned to Teri and she nodded. There was no chance anyone was going to sleep for a while and the kids were wide awake. We led the kids towards the bar along with the vast majority of the guests to settle our nerves. I don't think I'd ever seen it so busy.

I got the kids a glass of lemonade each and Teri and I shared a Bacardi and coke to calm our nerves.

The camaraderie around the hotel bar was wonderful and it was typical of the English mentality. This was the time when total strangers started talking to each other and in times of adversity friends were being made. I even chatted to one of the Union Jack brigade; he actually seemed like a decent guy. Then his wife shouted in a very loud West Midlands accent across the bar that he might as well get her two pints of lager to save him going back to the bar again for a little while. I raised my eyebrows and looked sideways at Teri. She smiled back at me and I sensed she was thinking along the same lines. I couldn't be sure of course, but I was certain that the words *planet* and *knob-head* were included in her thought process.

We sat around a table with the family of cockney ladies and I introduced them properly to Teri and the kids.

'How's the book going?' said one of the younger girls.

'Well, not too well actually. I've been busy doing things.'

She looked at Teri, arched one eyebrow and cheekily said, 'yes I can see!'

Teri blushed slightly even though she was at that point with the alcohol when you feel bullet proof. I felt I needed to defend her honour and made it clear that we were just very good friends and when I'd said I'd been busy it was just spending time with the three of them.

'Well as long as you've had a good time Ed.' she answered.

I smiled and said that it had been very good. I went on to tell them that we were planning on meeting back in the UK in a week or so.

'Good for you both.' came the reply from Sue, the mother of the group. 'If you don't mind me saying you make a nice couple.'

It was my turn to blush and at the same time I managed an awkward smile.

It was about 11.30 and several of the families with younger children started to disperse. I looked at Teri who was obviously thinking along the same lines herself.

'Time for bed?' I enquired, gesturing towards the children. It was clear that Teri hadn't witnessed the gesturing, only the words because she quickly looked at her children and turned to me with a look of horror in her eyes.

I quickly cottoned on that she'd got the wrong end of the stick and again gestured towards the children and reiterated the previous question in a slightly different way: 'Are the kids ready for bed?'

Mattie gave a sigh and squeezed his face showing everyone the lines on his forehead. Lucy just yawned in agreement with me. Teri simply closed her eyes and nodded.

So it was time to take the kids to bed. I carried Lucy for half of the way back to their room and Mattie for the remaining way.

When we arrived back at the room Teri looked at me with more than a hint of resignation and the clear message in her eyes said, *'it's not going to happen tonight.'* After several nights of near misses I was resigned to that very fact.

'You know it's going to take quite a while for the kids to settle.' Teri said.

I assured her that I understood and went on to say that it would take quite a while for me to settle too.

'I can see that you need time to sort things out.' I said, 'I'll leave you guys to it. I'll catch you tomorrow.'

Teri thanked me for my understanding and kissed me lightly on the cheek before wishing me goodnight.

I made my way back to my room in a state of contemplation. So many questions were forming in my head: 'How much did I really like Teri?'

'How much did I still want Marie?'

'How drunk was I right now?'

The answer to all three questions was the same word: *'VERY!'*

In my current state the only question that mattered now was the first one. I couldn't change how drunk I was right now, it was much too late for that and I certainly couldn't do anything about Marie. Whatever I still felt about her was irrelevant, because it was utterly and completely out of my hands!

Chapter Eighteen

What I've come to realise is that the Cyprus sun can do strange things to your head. People who you really don't know that well can seem like old friends. Things can be blown out of all proportion and you can seriously embarrass yourself. And that's exactly what I was just about to do. It went something like this:

'Teri, I have something I need to tell you.' I said a little apprehensively. I could feel the anxiety building within me as I added, 'you might have a little clue what it is.'

'Oh I might, might I?' she replied in a rhythmical almost symmetrical way.

My heart was starting to pound in my chest. I could feel the beads of sweat on my forehead and my throat felt instantly dry.

'Well I hope so yes, it's about us.'

'That's a relief; I thought you were coming out or something.'

'*Go on tell her,*' the voices said in unison. '*Tell her how you feel*'

'Teri, it's like this. Shit, I don't know how to say it. I think I've fallen for you.'

'Several times this week if I recall!' she joked.

'It's about what we discussed the other night.' As I was mouthing the words I hoped I'd not already blown it.

'Remind me Ed, we talked about all sorts of things if I remember.' she said a little nervously.

'Well, we said we'd maybe continue seeing each other back in the UK.' Teri's head turned a little to one side and both eyebrows were raised a little.

'But, you don't mean actually **seeing** each other do you? Isn't **that** just a bit too soon, don't you think?'

For a brief moment I thought about my answer and then said it out loud: 'Not for me.'

'Well Ed, if you haven't noticed, it's slightly different for me, what with the kids and my study and all.'

'What are you saying Teri? I'm going home later today and I thought that…well, I thought that we…' I couldn't find the rest of the words.

Then she put me out of my misery.

'Ed I like you, I like you a lot. But this is crazy. We've known each other a matter of days. It's crazy don't you think?' Her eyes pleaded with me to agree. I couldn't.

'Teri, I know what I want, and I know that I want to carry on seeing you.'

A strained smile broke out on her face and I could see the sadness in her eyes. 'Ed, you've already told me you're an *all* or *nothing* guy. I'm afraid to say as much as I would want to; I can't give you what you want right now.'

'Okay, I get the picture, no worries.' I said defensively.

'There you go again, I said, **right now**, I can't give you what you want right now. It's all too soon for me. You'd need to give me some time?'

'Well, how much time?' I pleaded, 'how long do you need?'

'I don't know. You've just laid this on me and trust me Ed I don't need this shit right now.'

I was starting to get a little annoyed. 'Oh its shit now is it? Teri it's simple it's *all* or *nothing*. What's it to be?'

'Okay *nothing* then.' She then turned and walked away without looking back.

I couldn't believe this was how it was ending. I thought she really liked me. I thought we'd at least catch up with each other when we got back to the UK. After all she only lived half an hour or so up the road, it was nothing.

We'd got on so well. I asked myself was it all a fake, was I imagining everything, was it just a holiday romance? These were all questions that I didn't have an answer to. But they had one thing in common; they made me feel so very empty inside. I was feeling sad and even a little angry. There was no doubt about it I felt like the biggest idiot in Cyprus.

Looking back I was certainly *acting* like the biggest idiot on the island, but hindsight as they say is a wonderful thing.

What was left of my holiday on the *island of love* was miserable. I kept myself to myself and avoided all contact with other human beings. The thought of seeing Teri was too painful to contemplate.

I was already packed and ready to go hours before the coach arrived. Nothing new there then. Dad again.

The coach taking us back to the airport arrived and I boarded it very quickly keeping my head down. At the last moment I looked up to see Teri and the kids waving at me. I squeezed out a smile and waved back to them. I could just make out a few words she was miming at me. One was *goodbye*; the other was *thank-you*.

All I could manage to do in return was to wave very slowly in a regal like manner. It must have looked quite pathetic but the tears in my eyes and the lump in my throat made anything else impossible.

The flight home was incident free. The landing was smooth and we all applauded. I collected my case and dug out the car park form. The car started first time and I was grateful for small mercies. The drive home was a blur and I hated every single minute. I was tired and emotionally shattered and I felt like my heart was broken in two.

I had the next day off to get on top of things. It took several hours to sort out the mail, chuck a couple of loads in the washer, and loads of other stuff.

I was trying not to think too much about the holiday. Whenever my mind slipped back to Cyprus I could feel the knot in my stomach.

The following day I was back at work, running my empire! I was as busy as hell and right now was extremely thankful for the diversion from my thoughts of Cyprus. I was still feeling pretty sorry for myself.

A couple more days passed by and I started to seriously regret how I'd handled everything and how I'd put Teri under so much pressure. Why did I have to be so heavy with her? Why did I have to be such a first rate plonker? It was while I was having one of these self tormenting moments when my phone made that sound that indicated an incoming text.

I looked instantly to see who the sender was and my heart skipped a beat. It was from Teri. It simply said: *'Home now. It was lovely to meet you. I hope you're well. The kids miss you. So do I. Teri. X'*

I toyed with what to say in response and then in a moment of inspiration I had it, I wouldn't send a reply at all.

I would phone her instead.

I composed myself and dialled the number she'd given me. The phone rang five times and then there was a second's silence.

Missing the Plot

'Hello? Teri?' I said a little nervously.

'Hi.' was her reply. 'Is that Ed?'

'Yeah, how are you? How are the kids?'

'Good, we're all good, what about you?'

'I'm fine thanks, err Teri; I need to tell you something…'

I suddenly realised I didn't know what the hell to say to her. My heart was beating fast and I could feel the blood rushing in my veins. For some reason I was nervous and almost lost for words. If I'd had time to think about it, I would have rehearsed what I wanted to say. I'm a sales professional and sometimes you stand in front of the mirror and practice your presentation so that the right words come out in the right order and show you off in the best possible light. I realised it was a little too late for that and I needed to get to the point.

'Teri I want to apologise for being such an idiot. I realise that I was asking too much and I want to thank you for everything. I think you and the kids are great. How do you feel about meeting up one day for a coffee or something?'

'Ed, that's a nice idea, but… listen, you're a great guy. Do you mind if I say something personal?'

I was intrigued and said, 'sure, go ahead.'

'Ed, if you don't mind me saying I still think there's a real chance for you and your wife. Ed it's obvious you still love her. You should maybe try again.'

'It's not that easy Teri; there's been a lot of water under the bridge. You can't turn back the clock.'

'Ed, how do you really feel? What do you truly want?'

I was silent for several seconds and simply replied, 'to be happy again.' Tears were filling my eyes and I knew for the first time in a long time that I still desperately loved my wife. Teri had sensed that I was kidding myself, I hadn't moved on from Marie. We'd been separated for over a year but had never taken it any further. Something had held us back. Some force had prevented us from breaking up completely. Teri had known that it was crazy for me to jump into another relationship with someone else. She knew we would both get hurt.

'Thank you Teri, thank you for everything. I'll never forget you.'

She simply said, 'take care and good luck.'

The phone went silent and my tears became heavier, but this time they were tears of joy.

Chapter Nineteen

After yesterdays' conversation with Teri it was clear that I needed to think about what to do next, I needed a plan of attack. Marie and I had been separated for well over a year, but we were still very good friends. I still thought the world of her and deep down I knew she felt the same about me. We'd obviously been through a terrible time this last year or so and the six months before we separated, when things started to fall apart.

But after all we'd been through, if we still felt so strongly towards each other then surely there was some hope. My heart and every bone in my body certainly hoped so.

I had been the one who'd made serious enquiries about divorce, which at the time Marie had vigorously tried to dissuade me from taking such drastic action.

After much soul searching in the end I made a complete turnaround and put the divorce proceedings on hold, in fact it was just before the Cyprus trip.

I awoke one morning to the stark reality of the situation and I realised I was making a rash decision and though I couldn't possibly know how the future would unfold I felt that divorce at that time was definitely the wrong thing for me.

I decided to speak to a good friend of mine to discuss the matter. I arranged to meet him for lunch and we went to a lovely little Bistro on the edge of Nottingham. We had discussed my relationship and predicament many times over the last two years and to be fair he had always said that if we could get back together and make a fresh start then that was the path to go down. He always felt it would be a difficult path, but not impossible. We ordered a light lunch each and a few drinks and I bought him up to speed on things. He listened intently and asked if I minded if he told me bluntly what he thought. I invited him to go ahead by saying, 'Will, that's why I'm talking to you. I know you'll give it to me straight.'

'Okay then, simple question Ed, do you still love her?'

'Absolutely!'

'Okay, that's good. Do you still want her?'

'Without doubt.'

'Well what are you pissing about for then, you arse!'

It was fiercely blunt, but it was directly on the mark. I shrugged my shoulders and talked about needing to go to the end of my journey, needing to get to the point I was now at.

'Well now you've got there, stop pissing about.'

'YES SIR!' I said at the same time as saluting him. We ordered a coffee and I of course footed the bill. As we parted I thanked him for his company and his honest views. His final words to me were, 'you've got a chance Ed, don't cock it up.'

I assured him I'd try not to.

Later that evening I was reflecting on our conversation and there was no doubt Will was right, it was time for me to be decisive and has he put it so succinctly, *stop pissing about.*

I was going to take the bull by the horns and contact Marie in the morning.

That night was full of broken sleep, full of dreams of times gone by and thoughts of things that still might be. In the morning I helped myself to a large bowl of cereal topped with a chopped banana and a mug of coffee to follow. I spent an hour in the office checking emails and doing some paperwork. The time was now 9.45 and I figured that Marie would be up and at it. She didn't work on Fridays but was normally up by 9am on her days off. I scrolled down the contacts list on my mobile phone to *"M"*. I then found Marie's mobile number and pressed the green button to make the call. The telephone rang, my heart began to race, the telephone rang again, and a million things went through my mind. What am I going to say again? I'd rehearsed it all last night but my mind had suddenly gone very blank and I knew I'd be lost for words. The telephone rang seven times, each time

I braced myself for an answer. It never came. The answer machine message kicked in: 'Hi, this is Marie, I can't take your call right now, but please leave your message and I'll call you back as soon as I can.' As the message was playing I thought about what to say, by the end of the message I'd decided not to say anything, just to hang up. I'd call again later.

Anyway what message would I leave? 'I want you back,' or 'I still love you and want to try again.' No, I think it was best for me to call later and try to find the right words in the right order to make my feelings known.

I had a meeting at 11.30 in Mansfield with one of my clients and needed to get a move on. After a quick shave and shower I was suited and booted and ready for action. I was conscious that if I set off at 10.15 I would be at least half an hour too early for the appointment. Nonetheless I set off on my journey knowing I was going to be annoyingly early. I convinced myself that there could be some sort of traffic hold up along the way and it was better to be too early than a little late. Dad, you've got a lot to answer for.

During the meeting I put my phone on silent; I always considered it rude to take a call during a business meeting. I didn't appreciate it when people answered their mobile phone in meetings and I always made it a rule not to be what I considered unprofessional in front of my clients.

When I got back to the car I checked my phone and could see that I'd missed two calls. The first was from another one of my clients and the second was from Marie. I was instantly filled with an icy numbness which spread throughout my body; the hairs on my arms were standing to attention on the end of a thousand goose bumps. Why was she calling me? *'She was returning your call you fool.'*

I shook my head and felt I needed to collect my thoughts before calling her back. Two minutes later my thoughts felt suitably collected and I made the call. After seven rings the answer machine kicked in again and once again I decided to hang up. So far it wasn't going to plan, but I was adamant that I wasn't going to leave a message; I knew that sooner or later we would connect.

I returned the other missed call and arranged a meeting with the client for the following Tuesday, they wanted to look at changing their ad. They asked me to think about some ideas over the weekend and we'd discuss them at the meeting. It was a part of the job I loved, coming up with new ideas. It was a bit of a gift, something I was pretty good at. You had to be good at something I guess.

I headed back home and thought about Marie and what I was planning to say when we eventually spoke, which would hopefully be soon. I called at the supermarket and bought a few essentials for a Friday night in, namely some bottles of lager, a bottle of Chardonnay and a microwavable Chicken

Tikka Masala. Not really a balanced diet, but a typical *end of week* treat. I arrived back home and put a couple of bottles of Bud in the freezer. I was in need of a cold beer pretty soon. I popped upstairs and heard the familiar beeping sound of the answer machine, indicating a message. I pressed the play button to reveal Marie's voice, 'hi love, it's only me. I've been trying to call you on your mobile. I've missed a few calls from you earlier. I'll catch you later. But don't forget I'm out with Amy and Sarah tonight and I'm staying over. See you soon.'

Shit I'd forgotten about that leaving do. I resigned myself to calling Marie the following day and chewed over in my mind what I was going to say to her when we spoke. The trouble was, I knew that no matter how much I practiced the words, they would sound so very different when I said them for real.

There was nothing else for it, I needed a drink. I grabbed myself a bottle of the now freezing cold lager and flipped off the top. Not for the first time of late I sank it in one without touching the sides. I put the oven on and started to prepare the meal, which just entailed taking it out of the box and pricking the plastic sleeve. I was becoming quite accomplished in the kitchen!

Throughout the evening I was restless and just couldn't relax. I'd play pool for ten minutes and then flick through the channels on the TV, then I'd find something of interest and stay with it for five minutes before playing some more pool. I'd then get bored and return to the TV for more surfing on the hundred or so channels I had. There were old comedies, old movies, old dramas and old documentaries. Every one of them repeats. My problem was that I'd seen most of them before. I'd spent an awful lot of time in the last year or so in front of the goggle box, usually with a glass of wine or a bottle of beer for company. I settled on an old Bruce Willis film I'd seen many times, the Fifth Element. Even as I started to watch it I knew every scene, most of the dialogue and certainly how it would end. I was comforted by the thought of the happy ending, although I felt pretty certain I wouldn't actually see the ending tonight. I was starting to feel a heaviness in my eyes and I knew I was going to fall asleep long before that wonderful final scene when Bruce kisses the heroine, tells her he loves her and she saves the world. I watched the film for about ten more minutes and then slowly began to fade into numbness. Within seconds my eyes were closed and sleep became my master. The Fifth Element continued to play on into the night without me.

As ever when I'd fallen asleep in front of the television I awoke in the middle of the night feeling cold and stiff. For a moment or two I was confused and disorientated, but my eyes quickly adjusted to the surroundings, my tired brain soon caught up and I dragged my weary body upstairs

Missing the Plot

and soon fell back into a deep sleep in the comfort of my bed.

Chapter Twenty

The next day I awoke with a touch of a hangover that was soon gone after two paracetemol and a hearty breakfast. I needed a clear head because this was definitely going to be the day I poured out my heart to Marie. This was going to be the day I told her how I felt and that I wanted us to try again. I was nervous at the response she would give. There was no guarantee that she would want the same thing. There was no doubt that we still had strong feelings for each other, but that didn't mean we could make a go of our marriage. However, whilst I knew there had been a lot of water under the bridge during these past two years, I felt that the water hadn't washed away our love. In fact more recently I was starting to feel that the water had actually cleaned away some of the crap, certainly from my point of view.

I composed a text message to suggest that we could get together for a coffee or maybe even lunch later. In the text I also said I had something interesting to ask her. I knew she would have been intrigued. Through past experience I knew it didn't take much to get her thinking. It was 10.30am and whilst I was sure it was still too early for Marie on a Saturday after a night out I decided to send it anyway. I checked the spelling and grammar, as if it mattered and I pressed the send button. As I did so I caught my reflection in the mirror. I looked tired and decidedly rough. If I was going to make a good impression then I needed to smarten myself up. It was time for a shave and a shower. Something I rarely did on a Saturday morning, but this was no ordinary Saturday morning. This was potentially one of those life changing days and I wanted to look my best. As I headed upstairs I once again looked in the mirror and frowned at myself. One thing was apparent; if I wanted to look my best I needed an overhaul, in fact by the look of me, a major one.

Sometime later the miracle I needed to happen was complete, thanks mainly to having a good shave and a long hot shower. I thought about what I was going to wear to this meeting and suddenly realised that we hadn't actually arranged to meet yet.

The text! I wondered if she'd replied while I was in the shower. I raced downstairs and sure enough there was a message in the inbox. I pressed to reveal who it was from and to my nervous delight it was from Marie. It read: 'Busy today, but can pop for half an hour at teatime.'

It seemed Marie was always busy on a Saturday, always catching up with friends and family. When not visiting she'd be shopping for something or usually returning something that didn't quite fit her as well as she thought when she'd tried it on the previous weekend. Women eh!

I thought about what to reply in the text and decided on the following: 'Hiya, hope you had a good night. Regarding today, shall we say 5.30 then? Ed. X'

I pressed the send button and seemingly within seconds the phone beeped as a message arrived saying, 'that's great. See you later. Have a good day. X.' Now all I had to do was kill the six hours between now and then.

I was instantly bored and decided to pack my bag and visit the local gym.

I knew that I'd be just as bored there, but at least it would pass a few hours. At the gym I followed my usual exercise routine, forty five minutes worth of aerobics, loads of sit ups and a round of various weight machines. There were several characters that made me smile and it was a bit like the poolside at the hotel in Protaras. There were fat people, desperately trying to lose weight and of course the muscle bound crew that seemed to gather in groups and watch in turn as their mates pressed weights. After a time everyone got the chance to have a go pumping iron as the gang of biceps and triceps happily watched each other work up a sweat. One guy in particular had a huge chest and an even larger gut. It seemed he had built up a lot of bulk on his upper body, but had neglected any effort to work on his lower abdomen.

The result looked hilarious and the humour for me was further enhanced by his Elvis Presley quiff. Every time he walked by me I couldn't help sticking up one side of my upper lip and whispering an Elvis style *"thank-you very much"* under my breath. On one occasion a lady to the side of me turned and smiled, I think she understood my thinking. However, I was careful not to mock him too loudly; because he was built like Garth, that old comic strip hero from the Daily Mirror. Though it had to be said that in this world, Garth was not only barrel chested, he was barrel bellied too!

After the gym I did a bit of shopping at the nearby supermarket and decided I'd buy a nice card for Marie. It was a card for a special friend. Inside I wrote the words: 'The flame still burns.' I simply signed it *'Love Ed'* and a big kiss. I grabbed a sandwich and an orange juice from the cooler and packed the shopping in the car.

I always kept my golf clubs in the boot and I was now heading for the driving range to hit a few balls. Golf is a game that really keeps your feet on the ground. Even the best golfers in the world are often kept in check by this so called simple game of hitting a little ball with a series of metal clubs towards a hole. All you had to do then was to sink your ball into the hole. It couldn't be easier, right?

I hit fifty balls and not one shot was the same. The balls went left, right, high, low and never handsome.

I was learning the game and it was early days, but I looked on with a measure of envy at the guy to the left of me who hit shot after shot right down the middle to the same spot of the range.

Then I realised he was the local golf professional and I didn't feel so bad, especially when most of the other people on the range were of a similar standard to me, which could best be described as the *"shit"* side of poor.

Still at least I was passing more time and it was now only a few hours to go until Marie arrived for our little chat. My hands instantly started to sweat and I felt a little queasy. I knew I needed to keep myself occupied for the last two hours of waiting. If I didn't I knew the two hours would seem like ten. I headed home with the intention of mowing the lawn. That normally took me about an hour and a half. Perfect timing.

I put my work clothes on and proceeded to work up my usual sweat trudging up and down the lawn. I filled about five big black bags and it was as usual hard work as the back lawn was about a quarter of an acre.

I was just putting the mower away when I heard a voice I recognised calling my name, it was Marie. *'Shit.'* I thought, *'she's early. She's NEVER early!'*

Sure enough for first time in twenty odd years Marie was early for something. She had arrived at the point were I looked shattered and completely covered in fragments of grass cuttings and dripping in sweat, so much for the perfect timing!

'You're early.' I said.

'Yeah I know. You don't mind do you?' I shook my head and said I didn't mind at all but inside I was thinking quite the opposite. This wasn't the first impression I'd wanted to give. But it was too late now; she'd seen me in all of my sweaty glory. I suggested that she put the kettle on while I had a quick shower. She agreed.

I dashed upstairs to have a hot shower and within a few minutes was back downstairs again to be greeted with a mug of steaming coffee and a couple of digestives. 'Cheers love.' I said with genuine appreciation. We stepped outside and sat at the patio table to drink our coffee and eat our biscuits.

'So what did you want to ask me?' Marie enquired. I dunked one of my biscuits and just managed to get it to my mouth before it fell apart; I then took a large gulp of the hot drink and composed myself.

'Well Marie, it's like this, I want us to try again.' Marie was obviously shocked to hear these words and her jaw literally dropped leaving her mouth wide open.

She said nothing. I repeated the words just in case she didn't hear me properly the first time. She shuffled uneasily in her seat and sighed heavily.

'I can't believe you.' she said. 'You wanted a divorce last month and you were convinced it was over and you were moving on.' I shrugged my shoulders and explained that my feelings had changed and I now realised what I truly wanted and that was her. I went on to say that I'd put the divorce on hold before I went to Cyprus.

'Well, you could have told me that!' she said in disbelief. Then she slowly shook her head and sighed yet again, but not so heavily this time. 'Ed, I begged you to take me back and you pushed me away. I've had to move on myself.'

'I know, I'm sorry.' I said. 'But I needed time and I needed to complete *my* journey. It would have been too early for me. Don't you see?'

'Oh I understand Ed. It's just a shock to hear what you're saying.' She closed her eyes as if in deep thought and went on to say, 'I'll need to think about it for a few days.' I nodded and said that I expected that she would need some time to think. I went on to apologise for pushing her away but promised her that I was now ready to try again.

'Oh Ed.' she said, 'that's what I wanted all along. I just don't know if it's too late now.' A lump formed in my throat but I kept my composure and said, 'I hope not.'

Marie looked at her watch and said she was sorry but she had some plans for the rest of the day. Apparently she was going to a barbecue at one of her work friends at 5.30, which is why she had come early to see me. 'No worries.' I said. 'Have a nice time.'

'What have you got on?' she enquired with interest. I told her I was just chilling out, having a bite to eat and watching a bit of television. This was true, but I neglected to mention the large amount of alcohol I was also planning to consume.

I desperately needed something to dull my feelings, my good friends Mister Budweiser and Mister Shiraz would surely help. I walked her to her car and we kissed tentatively on the lips. She smiled. 'I'll be in touch. Have a nice evening.' She closed the car door and started the engine.

'You too.' I replied. She blew me a kiss and drove away. It hadn't gone quite as I'd planned it. But what did I expect? We had been apart for over a year and things weren't going to be back to normal overnight.

I resigned myself to the fact that it was very early days and that Rome wasn't built in a day. I would give Marie the space to think about what she wanted and hope she wanted the same as me. I walked back into the house and made my way straight to the fridge. It was time for a beer.

Chapter Twenty One

The following day I was determined to be positive. I was also keen not to rush Marie in any way. It was clear from our conversation yesterday that she needed some time to think about a very important decision. Yes it would have been nice if she had fallen into my arms and kissed me like she'd never kissed me before, but this wasn't a book, this was real life!

I knew I had to be patient. I was tempted to call her but I resisted the urge. I contemplated sending a text and even reached for my phone. But I realised that this really didn't give her the space she needed. Yes it's nice to know people are thinking of you, but clearly she needed room to breathe and to consider what and who she truly wanted.

I realised that I hadn't given Marie the card I'd bought her. It was left on the side in readiness, but because she'd arrived so early it had slipped my mind. However, I wasn't fazed in any way as I was sure I'd very soon get the opportunity to give it to her. My fingers were tightly crossed, along with my toes, my legs, my arms and strangely enough, even my eyes!

I decided to head for the gym again and take my mind off things. Sunday was a lot quieter and even the muscle bound crew were short of their usual numbers and I was disappointed to see that *"Elvis had left the building!"*

After my workout I went for a swim and then enjoyed ten minutes in the Jacuzzi. I sat there on my own and relished the warm water and the high powered jets massaging my back. I tried to think about something else, but found my thoughts slipping back to my wife and our marriage. It had been a really good marriage; we'd been very happy for most of it and had raised two wonderful children. We'd been the best of friends and were compatible in every way. I was always able to make her laugh, which they say is important in a relationship, and sometimes I even managed to do it intentionally. But most of the time it was the daft things I did and the embarrassing scenarios I got myself into that made her laugh the most.

There was the time we'd taken the kids out for a meal at a Little Chef near Nottingham. Sam, our son had gone off to the toilet and seconds later Marie had said, 'you'd better go with him Ed.' I followed him into the gents, or so I thought. Little did I know at the time but Sam had gone into the disabled toilet instead. On entering the gents' toilet I noticed that it was empty apart from one engaged cubicle. I naturally assumed it was Sam. Why wouldn't I?

At the top of my voice and with a very deep somewhat menacing tone I announced, 'THE BIG GUY'S HERE. I'M COMING TO GET YOU.' There was silence apart from the sound of someone clearing their throat. I suddenly had a bad feeling and crouched down to check that Sam was actually in there. What I saw was obviously not my son. I quickly exited the toilet and bumped into Sam who was coming out of the disabled toilet. The realisation hit me and I gently grabbed his arm and hurriedly rushed back to join Marie and our daughter Sarah at the table. I was already laughing as I relayed the story to the three of them and we all laughed as several minutes later a very timid looking elderly gentleman made his way very gingerly back from the toilets to join his wife. 'He looks frightened out of his wits.' Marie whispered and we all laughed again. Without further adieu I quickly paid the bill and we swiftly made our escape.

It was stories like this that had made our marriage a barrel of laughs. Yes the kids had moved on, but we still enjoyed each others company. The question in my mind was, *'would we ever get the chance to enjoy it again?'* I was suddenly aware that several people had joined me in the Jacuzzi and I immediately decided to leave them to it. It was time for me to change, and I don't just mean out of my swimming shorts and into my jeans and T-shirt!

I decided I would get some moral support from Tony and we agreed to meet for a coffee. As ever my best mate was full of joviality as we discussed the very latest twists and turns in my relationship.

'You know my thoughts mate. You and Marie are meant to be. Sometimes the path we take can be long and hard before we get to where we're supposed to be.'

'You should have been a philosopher Tone. You're full of bullshit!'

'All I'm saying is that sometimes it can be a difficult road, but the journey can be worth it in the end!'

'What is it with *you* and *roads*? You'll be singing *'the long and winding road'* next!'

He smiled and started to clear his throat in readiness before I quickly and firmly stopped him in mid flow. 'Shut the fuck up and decide on which cake you're having.' He smiled and pointed to the carrot cake. I turned to the lady serving us and said, 'two coffees and two carrot cakes please.'

We talked for a while and he didn't mention paths or roads once. I was grateful for small mercies.

'Seriously mate, you've got to give her some more time.' He said with real belief.

'Yeah I know mate and thanks.'

'Thanks for the good advice you mean?'

'No, thanks for not singing!' I said with a smile.

Once again we parted with a firm shake of hands and I felt much better than I'd felt for some while.

Friends are worth their weight in gold, which in Tony's case would be an awful lot of gold!

Even though I'd agreed with Tony's advice about giving Marie more time, as the day continued I was feeling ever more helpless. It felt like I was just *killing* time. But unlike yesterday there was nothing in particular I was working towards. I was just playing a waiting game until Marie was ready to give me a decision and with her track record over the last year or so that could take weeks. Still thankfully it was Monday tomorrow and I was always busy during the weekdays. I needed to iron some shirts for the week ahead and polish my shoes, which I did. I made myself a Sunday dinner and followed it my speciality dessert, what I called *posh* bananas and custard. You simply made some toffee by cooking some sugar in a pan, when it had caramelised you added a knob of butter and then you briefly tossed the chopped bananas in the pan for a few seconds; this coated them with the sweet toffee. It was then a case of adding some hot custard on top and the dessert was complete. I'd seen it done on one of those cookery programmes and it tasted as delicious as the celebrity chef in question had said it would. If nothing else this past year had made me into a dab hand in the kitchen.

I checked the TV paper to see what delights were in store for me later that evening and was happy to see that the programme about the SAS starring Ross

Kemp from Eastenders fame was on. I don't know exactly why but I always enjoyed that programme, and my mood lifted a little. At least it was something to look forward to.

The following week went by pretty quickly. It was a successful week and I managed to do lots of business and make lots of money. I never heard from Marie and I resisted the ongoing urge to contact her. However, I was getting more and more frustrated by the lack of an answer and at 3pm on Friday afternoon decided to test the water by sending a text. I enquired about her week and said that I hoped she was well. I ended the text with the words: 'See you soon. Love, Ed. X'

I waited for a reply but nothing came for over an hour. Just when I thought that Marie was obviously not going to reply or not able to reply, the phone beeped. The message said two words: 'Call me.' It was from Marie. I nervously scrolled down the recent calls list to find her number and pressed the green button. The phone rang. What was I going to say? It rang again. What was she going to say? It rang a third time and I could feel my heart begin to race. On the fourth ring she answered with, 'hiya love.'

'Oh hi.' I said in return. 'How are you?'

'I'm fine Ed.' She paused for a moment then continued. 'I've been thinking.' It wasn't time for joking but I couldn't help myself, it's one of my failings. 'I wondered was that noise was last night.'

'Funny!' she said. 'No, I've been thinking about what you said.'

'Okay.' I said with some apprehension, 'and what did you decide?'

There was another long pause and then she spoke, 'Ed I've been thinking and I need to ask you a few things, face to face.'

I nervously said okay and suggested that she come over and ask them. I can't make it tonight, but I'll pop tomorrow if that's okay?' I agreed and we settled on lunchtime, about 12.30. We said our goodbyes and finished the call. Questions were spinning around in my head. What did she want to ask me? Was she thinking of trying again? Was she going to tell me to my face that it was finally over between us? I realised that there was nothing I could do about it right now. It was just after 4.15 on Friday and probably far too early to have a beer. The sun was shining and the garden looked lovely and I convinced myself that it was the weekend after all. With that I cracked open a bottle of Bud and battled the voices in my head.

After another beer and a good half an hour in the sun I started to think about what I was going to do if Marie didn't want to try again. In that scenario

I wouldn't have much choice apart from getting on with my life. At that moment two things happened; firstly a voice inside started to give me a head-full of abuse because I'd already had the chance to try again and pushed her away and secondly my mobile phone rang. I grabbed it to see who was calling and was amazed and pleasantly surprised to see it was Teri. I answered it with a very enthusiastic, 'hello Teri.'

'Hi Ed, how are you? How are things?'

'Well, err, not so bad thanks, how about you?' I replied.

She went on to say that she was well and both kids were too. They'd been to the cinema to see the new Indiana Jones film and had really enjoyed it.

She added, 'I thought I'd call you to see how things were going with you and your wife.'

There was a moments' pause and I realised that it was now my turn to talk.

'Not so good.' I said, 'we've met a few times but as yet nothing's been sorted. We're meeting again tomorrow and she wants to ask me some questions. I've got a bad feeling about it.'

'It'll be fine I'm sure.' she said. 'She probably needs to know that she's still special to you and that you're not going back to her for the wrong reasons.'

'Well I'm not. I still really love her. It just took meeting you for me to realise it.'

'Thank you…..well I think I mean thank you.' she said.

I explained to Teri that meeting her had been wonderful and I was so very pleased that I had, because it made me realise that I still loved Marie with all my heart and that meeting Teri made me realise that I desperately wanted to try to make a life again with my best friend, with my soul-mate, with my wife!

'Well I'm pleased to have been useful.' Teri said. 'Ed, you obviously really love your wife so don't do what so many people do. Don't give up. Keep trying and give her time. You say it has to be *'all'* or *'nothing'*. Well for most women *neither* option is ideal. Sometimes *'all'* can be so suffocating. All relationships need some space to breathe.'

'Are you a marriage councillor?' I cheekily enquired.

'No Ed, I'm a woman!' she replied.

'You certainly are Teri and I'm sure you're right. Maybe I need to change my approach slightly.'

'Not too much Ed, just slightly. You're a nice guy so try not to lose that.'

'Thanks Teri.' I said with real feeling.

'You're welcome' she said warmly. With that she wished me luck and we said goodbye. I somehow knew that I would never see her again.

For several seconds I felt a wave of sadness wash over my body. For a moment I felt a lump form in my throat and my heart was filled with a deep melancholy and then somehow in another moment the feeling was gone.

Teri was right I had to be patient but also determined. I knew what I wanted now and I wasn't going to give up. Marie had broken my heart and I in turn had broken hers. The question was would we get the chance to make it up to each other?

I decided that I would call Marie and let her know how I felt. I wasn't going to come on heavy in any way, just let her know that I would give her all the time she needed. I would just let her know that I wanted more than anything to try to be a couple again when she was ready to do so.

Just as I was about to dial her number the telephone rang. I was amazed to see it was Marie. 'You'll never believe this, but I was just calling you.' I said with sheer amazement in my voice.

'If you remember it used to happen all the time. It's a connection of minds and souls.'

'Wow, well trust me it still works.' I said. 'Did you want me for something?' I asked with a slight nervousness in my voice.

'Yes, I wanted to talk to you about tomorrow, but you go first.' she said. This was it. I'd not really thought about what I was going to say. I'd usually think about what I was going to say in this type of situation far too much. I'd almost certainly over analyse it. But here and now the words came out with no prior rehearsal, just straight from my heart. 'Marie, you know me, I'm an all or nothing sort of guy.'

'Yes, I remember, go on.'

'Well, I've thought of an alternative.'

'Which is?' she questioned.

'**Something,** as in the thing between all and nothing. When it comes to you Marie I'd rather have *something* than nothing at all.

Does that make sense? I love you Marie and I want you back in my life. But if that means a little bit at a time for a while then I'll have to cope. It's the *nothing* I can't cope with.' The words were flowing. I had no idea whether they made any sense, no idea how Marie was feeling about them. I was on a roll and my words flowed straight from my heart. I went on: 'Wherever we've been in the past doesn't matter. What matters now is where we can still go. What we can still be. Together.'

There was a long silence. I thought I'd been cut off. I thought she'd hung up on me. Then I heard what sounded like sniffles on the other end of the phone. 'Marie, are you okay?'

'Yes, Yes I am?'

'Is *something* alright for you?' I asked very tentatively.

'Yes. Yes it is.' she replied with a little shakiness in her voice.

'Great, that's great.' I gathered myself for a second or two and asked, 'what did you want to say to me?'

She too composed herself for a brief moment and said, 'I was going to ask you if you fancied doing *something* tomorrow Ed. I thought we could do something together, like we used to.'

As I started to comprehend her words I could feel a build up of emotion filling my entire body. I managed to reply with three simple words: 'I'd love to.'

'And who knows Ed, in time there's no reason why *something* can't lead us back to *everything* again someday, don't you think?'

All I could say was, 'yes.' There was nothing else to say. Tears formed in my eyes and slowly started to fall down my face, but inside I was smiling.

Epilogue

I never managed to write my book in Cyprus. But I'll never forget the journey of self discovery I went through along the way and I'll never forget the many interesting people I met during that week in the sun, especially a beautiful Yorkshire lady and her two wonderful children. The friendship I found gave me the belief in myself that had been lost for so long. But more than anything it gave me hope for the future and helped me unlock the love in my heart.

I hope that one day I'll find the words to write my story, but until then I'll carry on living my life. I know that living my life is the most important thing right now. Marie and I are happier than we've ever been before. We know we're different people this time around, but we're not threatened by it, on the contrary we embrace the changes in each other. She was lost for a while and then I was lost too, but in the end we've found each other again and I thank God for that.

As I look back I know that something happened to me in Cyprus, something that will change my life forever. The whole experience sparked off a whole new chapter in my life, perhaps a whole new book. Life's funny like that.

Printed in the United Kingdom by
Lightning Source UK Ltd., Milton Keynes
136967UK00001BA/70-72/P